Dear Reader,

In 20 months Silhouette Romance will celebrate its 20th anniversary! To commemorate that momentous occasion, we'd like to ask *you* to share with us why you've chosen to read the Romance series, and which authors you particularly enjoy. We hope to publish some of your thoughtful comments during our anniversary year—2000! And *this* month's selections will give you food for thought....

In *The Guardian's Bride* by Laurie Paige, our VIRGIN BRIDES title, a 20-year-old heiress sets out to marry her older, wealthy— gorgeous—guardian. Problem is, he thinks she's too young.... *The Cowboy, the Baby and the Bride-to-Be* is Cara Colter's newest book, where a shy beauty reunites a lonely cowboy with his baby nephew...and lassoes love in the process! Karen Rose Smith's new miniseries, DO YOU TAKE THIS STRANGER?, premieres with *Wealth, Power and a Proper Wife*. An all-work-and-no-play millionaire learns the value of his marriage vows when the wife he'd suspected of betraying him suffers a bout of amnesia.

Rounding out the month, we have *Her Best Man* by Christine Scott, part of the MEN! promotion, featuring a powerful tycoon who heroically offers protection to a struggling single mom. In *Honey of a Husband* by Laura Anthony, an ex-bull rider returns home to discover his childhood sweetheart is raising *his* child— by another woman. Finally, rising star Elizabeth Harbison returns to the lineup with *True Love Ranch*, where a city gal and a single-dad rancher lock horns—and live up to the Colorado spread's name.

Enjoy!

Joan Marlow Golan

Joan Marlow Golan
Senior Editor Silhouette Romance

Please address questions and book requests to:
Silhouette Reader Service
U.S.: 3010 Walden Ave., P.O. Box 1325, Buffalo, NY 14269
Canadian: P.O. Box 609, Fort Erie, Ont. L2A 5X3

WEALTH, POWER AND A PROPER WIFE

Karen Rose Smith

Silhouette
ROMANCE™
Published by Silhouette Books
America's Publisher of Contemporary Romance

In loving memory of my mother,
Romaine Arcuri Cacciola, 1921-1995.

I love you and miss you, Mom.

 SILHOUETTE BOOKS

ISBN 0-373-19320-3

WEALTH, POWER AND A PROPER WIFE

Copyright © 1998 by Karen Rose Smith

This edition published by arrangement with Harlequin Books S.A.

Printed in U.S.A.

Books by Karen Rose Smith

Silhouette Romance

Adam's Vow #1075
Always Daddy #1102
Shane's Bride #1128
†*Cowboy at the Wedding* #1171
†*Most Eligible Dad* #1174
†*A Groom and a Promise* #1181
The Dad Who Saved Christmas #1267
‡ *Wealth, Power and a Proper Wife* #1320

*Darling Daddies
†The Best Men
‡ Do You Take This Stranger?

Silhouette Special Edition

Abigail and Mistletoe #930
The Sheriff's Proposal #1074

Previously published under the pseudonym Kari Sutherland

Silhouette Romance

Heartfire, Homefire #973

Silhouette Special Edition

Wish on the Moon #741

KAREN ROSE SMITH

was born in York, Pennsylvania. On her days off from school, she would spend time with her mother, a third-grade teacher. Sometimes she would listen to students read and help them, even when she wasn't much older than they were. It seemed only fitting that she chose teaching herself, after majoring in English and French. Karen remembers those days with her mother well, and as she gets older, realizes how precious those memories are, as are all the remembrances of the people she loved who have passed through her life.

Karen loves to hear from her readers. They can write to her at P.O. Box 1545, Hanover, PA 17331.

Dear Reader,

The three heroes—Christopher, Jud and Luke—in my
DO YOU TAKE THIS STRANGER? miniseries face
challenges that disrupt their lives. Friends as well as
cousins, they support each other as they discover a love
they never expected to experience.

In *Wealth, Power and a Proper Wife,* Christopher's wife,
Jenny, awakens from a coma with amnesia. She and
Christopher eventually learn that strangers can become
friends and lovers more than once in a lifetime.

Love, Honor and a Pregnant Bride takes cowboy
Jud Whitmore for a rough ride in the second book of the
miniseries, until he realizes giving his heart can be as
satisfying as marrying Mariah, who is carrying his child.

The third book in the trilogy, *Promises, Pumpkins and
Prince Charming,* is a true Cinderella romance, complete
with stepsisters, a "fairy" grandmother and Prince
Charming as a contractor!

This series was a joy and a challenge to write, and I hope
these romances tug on your heartstrings long after you
finish reading them!

All my best,

Karen Rose Smith

Prologue

Christopher Langston pushed open the door to his bedroom, a sense of foreboding overtaking him. Ever since he'd unlocked the front door and felt the unusual emptiness, his heart had pounded faster. Tonight he'd missed dinner again and gotten tied up in a meeting until midnight. Sometimes, Jenny worked in her office on the lower level until he got home. But he'd found only darkness and silence downstairs and assumed she'd gone to bed. Intending to wake her, he was determined to find out what was troubling her; she'd been pulling away from him for months. Last night after he'd told her about his proposed two-month trip to Europe, she'd grown much too quiet—even for Jenny.

When he walked into their bedroom, his chest tightened at the sight of the four-poster, cherry-wood bed, still perfectly made. He remembered the two hang-up calls within the last few weeks—one on a weekend, one late in the evening—and the day he'd caught his wife practically whispering into the receiver. But she'd hung up quickly, saying it was a salesman. He'd wanted to believe her because the alternative was too painful to contemplate.

As he scanned the room, he spotted a white envelope on the dresser, propped against a photograph of the two of them on their wedding day over four years ago. He stared at the picture. Jenny's beautiful black hair was a contrast against her white veil and gown, against his white tuxedo. The wind had whipped his blond hair over his forehead and the photographer had caught her reaching up to tenderly push it back.

What had happened to them?

He picked up the envelope with his name written across the front. She'd been in a hurry. His heart racing, he pulled out the sheet of linen stationery.

Christopher—
I have to go away for a few days. You won't be able to reach me. Please try to understand.

Jenny

Anger rose up inside him, followed by a sense of betrayal he'd never imagined he could feel. One thought tormented him as he reached for the phone—she'd run off with another man.

First he'd find her.

And then?

Could he ever forgive her?

Would she even want to be forgiven?

The anger surged again and he pushed the pain away.

April 14

The rain pelted Jenny's windshield in almost impenetrable sheets as she carefully drove along the winding road. A few more hours and she'd be back in Connecticut...with Christopher. She loved him so. She always had, ever since the moment she'd met him at her college graduation party. It hadn't mattered that he was seven years older than she was. Or that he'd been much more experienced. And yet she'd never been absolutely sure of his feelings.

Oh, there was plenty of chemistry between them.

But Christopher had always kept a part of himself removed and, from the moment of his proposal, she'd wondered if he wanted to marry her out of deep, abiding love or because she was socially acceptable and proper wife material for his position as CEO of his own financial services company in West Hartford.

All she'd ever wanted to do was please him and make him happy. For the past year that had seemed impossible. And for the past seven months....

She thought about the man who had hugged her less than an hour ago. She'd gotten to know him in such a short period of time. And now she had to face Christopher and tell him the truth—

Suddenly a blast of stormy wind buffeted her car at the same time her tires hit a deep puddle along the side of the road. The steering wheel slipped through her fingers as she hydroplaned over the water and screeched into a curve, trees rising up before her...

Chapter One

April 19

Christopher ran his hand over his face and his beard stubble, realizing he should shave and change clothes. He'd been sitting by Jenny's bedside in ICU for five days now, watching…praying…hoping she'd awaken from the coma, in torment because he still didn't know where she'd been or what she had been doing before she'd skidded off a wet road.

The call about her accident had come after four days of wondering, and searching, and experiencing more anger and frustration than he could ever remember feeling. But then the state police had notified him that her car had run off the road and crashed into a tree, and she'd been rushed to a hospital in Binghamton, New York. What the hell had she been doing on some back road in New York State?

He shouldn't ask the question and he shouldn't care

about the answer. Looking down at her, her black hair so dark against the white pillowcase, her face so pale, her forehead bruised and marked by a row of stitches below her hairline, he just wanted her to wake up and smile at him again as she used to. He hated seeing her attached to an IV, as well as a cardiac/pulmonary monitor which detected arrhythmia or respiratory distress. Nurses came in every hour to take vitals and to observe neurological signs for any changes or indications that she might be waking up. A physical therapist had also been working her muscles.

He'd provided for the best of care.

So aware of everything about her after days of waiting for any positive sign, he suddenly saw her fingers flutter on the sheet. Then miraculously, her arm moved. He held his breath as she turned her face toward him and opened her blue eyes.

Taking her hand, he murmured her name. "Jenny. Jenny, can you hear me?"

"Where...where am I?"

"You're in a hospital in Binghamton. You were in an accident—"

"Binghamton? But I was just at my graduation. How did I get to Binghamton? And...who are you? Where's my mother?"

Christopher's blood ran cold, and he knew something was terribly wrong. But maybe it was simply a passing haze. "Jenny, it's me. Christopher. I know I need a shave..."

Her gaze moved curiously over his face. "I don't know you. I don't understand what I'm doing here." She tried to sit up and as she did, her IV line pulled taut, the monitor beeped loudly, and she put her other hand to her head and closed her eyes.

Pushing the call button rapidly three times in succession, Christopher laid his hand on her shoulder. "Lie back, Jenny, until the doctor comes in."

The contact of his hand on her body, hardly covered by the thin cotton gown, was electric. She opened her eyes again, her confused gaze searching his face. "Who are you?" she repeated.

He realized she needed more than a name. "I'm your husband."

Shock replaced the confusion and, instead of lying back as he directed—as Jenny would have done, she said in a trembling voice, "Please get the doctor. Now."

Christopher was used to giving orders, not taking them. But as the nurse rushed in, he turned away from the panic in Jenny's eyes to find her doctor...and answers.

Less than an hour later, he paced the hall, every now and then glancing into the room where his wife's doctor was examining her. Just as he'd decided to barge into the room to watch and listen to Dr. Bartlett's evaluation firsthand, he saw a familiar face coming down the hall.

Luke Hobart was his cousin, but more important, his friend. He, Luke and another cousin, Jud, had spent summers together on their uncle's ranch in Texas. Christopher didn't see or talk to Jud as much as he'd like, especially since Jud had taken over running the Star Four for his father, but Luke lived outside of West Hartford and they managed to connect whenever their schedules allowed. He'd mentioned he'd try to drive to Binghamton to see how Jenny was doing. Christopher was glad he'd come.

Luke's casual attire of jeans and denim jacket, his brown

hair long on his neck, gave no indication he ran a multi-million-dollar foundation for his family. When he came up to Christopher, he clapped him on the shoulder. "How is she?"

"She just woke up. The doctor's examining her."

Luke's brows arched and he grinned. "That's terrific! Will she be able to go home soon?"

"She doesn't know who I am, Luke."

"What do you mean she doesn't know who you are?"

Christopher shoved his hands into his trouser pockets. "She doesn't know my name. She doesn't know I'm her husband!"

"You can't be serious. Amnesia only happens in books. Do you think she's trying to hide—"

At that moment, Jenny's doctor came through the door, his expression grave.

Christopher knew Luke had been about to put into words the suspicion nudging him, too. He looked to the doctor for the answers he needed.

"Mr. Langston, let's go down to the lounge where we can talk."

The doctor's voice was kind, but Christopher didn't want kindness right now. He wanted the facts. "We can talk right here. This is my cousin, and he can hear anything you have to say. Why doesn't my wife know who I am?"

Seeing Christopher's determination, Dr. Bartlett took his stethoscope from around his neck, folded it, and slid it into his pocket. "Your wife's bruised ribs will heal in a week or so, as will the stitches on her forehead, but the head trauma she sustained is another matter."

"In what way?"

"It's unpredictable, and we can't always assess whether the consequences are temporary or permanent."

Christopher's body went rigid as if he knew a severe blow was coming. "You mean she'll never remember I'm her husband?"

"I can't determine whether her loss of memory is a result of trauma from the accident or actual physical damage. It seems Jenny has retained everything about her life up to her college graduation. But she has no memory of any events after the ceremony. I suppose the two of you met after that?"

The significance of Jenny's last memories cut Christopher deeply. "We met the day after her graduation at a party her mother gave for her."

Dr. Bartlett cocked his head and studied Christopher. "Is there a reason she might not want to remember her relationship with you?"

"Now wait a minute," Luke cut in. "If you're suggesting…"

The doctor spoke directly to Christopher. "I'm suggesting that if you want to help your wife recover, you look at all the pieces as objectively as you can. Sometimes we can't separate the psychological from the physical."

"Could she be faking?" Christopher asked gruffly.

Dr. Bartlett's mouth tightened into a grim line. Finally he answered, "That young lady in there is in a panic because she believes she's twenty-one rather than twenty-six, because she doesn't know where she is or how she got here, because she has no memory of a man who says he's her husband. Now, I don't know why you think she'd want to fake all that, but her racing pulse and shallow respiration when she feels the panic are very real. We can't overload her with information, but rather have to let *her* set the pace.''

The implications of Jenny's memory loss hit Christopher. They had no relationship. They had no connection. All they had was a marriage that might not even be worth as much as the paper on which their marriage license was printed. ''When can I take her home?''

''I'm going to move her to a regular room shortly and keep an eye on her tomorrow. If everything goes well, she can leave on Sunday. But she keeps asking for her mother. It might be better if she went home with someone familiar.''

The doctor's words tightened Christopher's chest. ''Jenny's mother died two years ago. There is no other family. I'm all she has. She's coming home with me.''

Christopher's determined words echoed in his head as he stood before Jenny's door a few hours later. He was annoyed with himself for being nervous, frustrated because his thoughts were in turmoil, veering toward anger and a sense of betrayal one minute and the desire to see Jenny fully recovered and back home with him the next. He wanted to know why she'd left…whom she'd met or been with. But he knew he had to be patient. She couldn't answer his questions until she remembered their marriage.

And she would. He'd do everything in his power to help her remember so they could get on with their lives. He'd had a thorough discussion with Dr. Bartlett, explaining what had happened to Jenny's mother, asking innumerable questions, determining the best way to help his wife recover.

Pushing open her door, Christopher suddenly realized he

should have knocked. But he still couldn't accept the idea
he was a stranger to her.

She'd been moved from the critical care unit to the private room he'd requested for her. As he entered it, he saw
her sitting in a chair, staring out the window. When she
heard him, she shifted, her gaze meeting his. "Dr. Bartlett
told me my mother died two years ago while she was jog-
ging—from a congenital heart defect she never knew she
had. But he couldn't tell me anything else. Did I sell her
house? Did I keep anything of hers? I can't imagine just
letting go of everything I treasured all my life!"

Christopher tried to put himself in Jenny's place as he
saw the evidence of tears on her cheeks. Compassion for
her loss and her confusion overshadowed the turmoil he
battled with. He wanted to stroke her beautiful long wavy
hair, tell her everything would be all right. But he didn't
know what she'd accept from him.

So he sat on the edge of the bed, across from her chair,
keeping his arms by his sides, and remembered the process
of settling her mother's estate. Jenny's father, who'd died
when she was a teenager, had been a doctor. Her mother
had been a lawyer. Even so, there had been a considerable
mortgage and debts to pay, leaving only a small inheritance
for Jenny. "We sold your mother's house. We really had
no choice. You took your time sorting and saving and giving away. We put her bedroom suite in one of our guest
rooms, and you kept her jewelry chests and crystal and a
closet full of personal items. You also kept all the things
of your father's that your mother had held dear. It's all in
our house, Jenny."

"Our house." She shook her head. "Dr. Bartlett said
you want me to come home with you."

"I think you'll regain your memory faster if you do. You really have nowhere else to go."

"But I don't *know* you. I can't be your wife when I don't remember marrying you!"

There was such a wall between them—a different kind of wall than the one that had risen between them the last few months. Still, in spite of it, he leaned toward her and felt the intense attraction that had always sparked between them. "I think you *do* know me, Jenny. Deep down where it counts."

The silence emphasized his words as her gaze searched his face side to side, up and down, every line and angle as if she were probing deep inside for recognition. "You shaved," she said quietly.

He'd also changed his shirt and eaten a decent meal with Luke—his first in the past five days. "I thought if I looked respectable, I could convince you to come home with me a bit easier."

A cautious smile tipped up her lips. "At least you're honest."

"I always try to be."

When she tilted her head, she was the Jenny he remembered—the woman he desired more than any other. But then she spoke, and he realized his memories might never be real again. "Do I have my own money? Do I have the photography studio I always wanted?"

Jenny had graduated from college with a liberal arts degree, but her avid interest had been photography. Yet she'd never told him she wanted her own studio, although they'd built a darkroom in the basement. "The money from your inheritance is invested. You never needed to work because I'm successful. Photography hasn't been a major interest the past couple of years. You do a lot of charity work...with my mother.''

''What do you do?'' she asked after absorbing everything he'd said.

''I'm a financial markets analyst and CEO of my own firm.''

''So...if I *didn't* want to go home with you, I don't have my own money to get an apartment.''

There were sparks of defiance in Jenny's eyes he'd never seen there before. ''You have your own checking account.''

''But you provide the funds for it.''

His wife didn't question him like this. His wife didn't argue with him. ''Yes, I provide the funds. Just as my father provides for my mother. You never had a problem with that. And as far as an apartment goes, you wouldn't have familiar surroundings there or the stimulus you need to remember. Or don't you *want* to remember?'' His suspicions that she would rather wipe the slate clean for reasons of her own were stronger than ever.

''I don't *know* if I want to remember. I don't know if I want to go to a strange house...with a strange man....''

He could hear the panic in her voice and the fear. For a moment he forgot his suspicions about her being unfaithful and only remembered the day they'd met, their nights of passion, the life they'd built. Taking her hand in his, he said gently, ''The house is large. The bedroom door has a lock. I can move my things to a guest room. If it will make you feel safer, I'm sure Pauline would stay in the house at night.''

''Pauline?''

''Pauline is our housekeeper. She and her husband, Fred,

live in the carriage house at the stables. He tends the horses and the property.''

Jenny pulled her hand away from his. ''Dr. Bartlett said I might never remember.''

Did she find his touch repulsive? Even with his doubts, the anger at her leaving, he was still attracted to her, and he thought he'd felt the same old sparks from her. He stood and went to the window, trying to keep everything in perspective. ''Dr. Bartlett also said your memory could come rushing back without any warning. Would you want to be alone if it does? You just awakened from a coma. You don't know yet if you'll have physical repercussions like headaches or dizziness. Pauline can make sure you recuperate properly if you're not comfortable with me.''

He stared out the window to give her time to think.

''Mr. Langston?''

He turned. ''Christopher.''

''All right. Christopher. I'll come home with you. It's the only reasonable thing to do. For now.''

For now.

It seemed that ''now'' was all they had.

On Sunday morning, Jenny paced back and forth across her room, restless and anxious to be discharged. She felt stronger today. Her ribs still hurt, but they would heal. It was hard to believe that just the day before yesterday, she'd been in a coma. Feeling sometimes as if she were walking through a dream, she couldn't quite grasp everything the doctor and Christopher Langston had told her since then. Whenever she thought of her mother...

Tears came to her eyes as sadness and loss again washed over her. Her mother was gone. She'd lost her father when she was sixteen. That grief had been tempered by having her mother to remember with, to understand, to hug. Trying to comprehend that she'd never see her mother again or walk through the house where she'd grown up seemed impossible.

Impossible. A word that was becoming very familiar to her. Wasn't it also impossible that she could be married to a man like Christopher Langston and not remember? He emanated such authority, such determination, such…sex appeal. His hair was the color of a lion's mane, his facial features strongly defined, especially the line of his jaw. His lips… She grew hot as she remembered him capping her shoulder when she'd awakened and later the feel of her hand in his. The excited tingling that had rushed through her fingers had made her pull away. So had other things.

His deeply dark-brown eyes sent mixed messages, one moment expressing his concern, the next an anger she felt more than saw or heard. He hadn't touched her yesterday— just visited, watched her carefully, and described where they lived in West Hartford. She'd felt awkward with him and guessed he hadn't felt any more comfortable than she had. When he'd returned again last night, he'd brought her magazines to help her catch up with what had happened in the world that she didn't remember. But as she'd turned the glossy pages, seeing actors and politicians, she'd been much too aware of Christopher Langston who'd studied her every reaction.

A sound alerted her to the door opening and she looked up, expecting to see a nurse who would do a final vitals check. But instead of a woman in a white uniform, the man who said he was her husband strode in, a canvas bag in his hand.

Jenny reached for the back of her gown that flew open with the slightest movement or draft and scrambled into the bed, covering herself with the sheet.

His lips twitched at her attempt at modesty. "We're married, Jenny. I've seen you in less than that gown before."

"Maybe if you didn't have all your clothes on, I wouldn't feel as awkward," she returned before she thought better of it. As it was, he looked tall and strong and entirely too virile in a cream polo shirt and camel slacks.

He looked surprised for a moment, then teased, "Would you like me to take my shirt off?"

She felt her cheeks flush as she realized she'd very much like to see his bare chest. Telling her imagination to behave, she answered, "I'd prefer some real clothes. I can't leave in this...."

Lifting the bag, he set it on the bed by her feet. "My mother sent these for you. My father just dropped them off."

"Your father?"

"He flew in this morning. He pilots his own plane. We thought it would be better for you to fly home rather than ride in a car for hours."

"Do you always make decisions for me?" she asked, not liking the feel of someone controlling her life. Maybe because she felt as if she had such little control right now.

His jaw tensed. "I was thinking about your comfort."

"I don't know if I like the idea of a small plane."

"You've flown with Dad before. He's a good pilot."

"I don't remember..."

Christopher came closer to the bed. "*Because* you don't remember, you're going to have to trust me."

Closing her eyes, she took a deep breath before opening them again. Then she murmured, "Trust takes time."

"It also takes practice. Let's start with the plane ride," he suggested reasonably.

She was going to have to get used to jumping in with

both feet. Her circumstances left her no choice. "All right. We'll start with the plane ride."

With a nod at the bag, he said, "Mother pulled these from your closet."

Clothes from a life she couldn't remember. Maybe if she recognized them... Reaching into the carryall, she pulled out a mint-green sweater and slacks. She held them in her hands, concentrating...hoping. But they were just clothes that she needed to wear, to a home she didn't remember.

Christopher sat on the bed next to her, his hip brushing her thigh. "Dr. Bartlett said not to push it, Jenny. Trying too hard to remember could prevent it from happening."

"But he also said anything could be a trigger."

"He gave me the name and number of a neurologist in West Hartford. He's already referred you. We'll do everything we can to help you recover."

The concern on Christopher's face was as real as the compassion in his voice. He looked tired, and she realized he'd been through a difficult time, not knowing the outcome of her condition. Yesterday, they'd acted like polite strangers, but if she was going home with him, she needed to know more about him...and herself.

Trying out the name he'd told her to use, she said, "Christopher, I'm sorry all of this has happened. I know it's difficult for you, too. I have so many questions about everything. About you. About us. Where was I going? What was I doing in Binghamton?"

The concern and compassion vanished, replaced by a coldness she hadn't seen there before. "Some of your questions only you can answer," he said. "No one else can." The few moments of feeling close to him disappeared as he stood. "Go ahead and get dressed. I'll try to hurry the paperwork."

When he left her room, Jenny felt more confused than

ever—as if she knew him…as if she didn't. Intuition told her that if she wasn't careful, he could be a dominating force in her life. For some reason, that thought bothered her.

She would go home with him. But she would tread carefully.

Leaves on the silver maples reflected the bright April sun as the limousine wended its way up the tree-lined driveway to the stately brick-and-stone house. Jenny was no stranger to fine things, but she suddenly realized that Christopher Langston was more than successful. He was quite wealthy.

Christopher's father, Wayne, who'd expertly piloted the plane and reassured her about his competency several times, smiled at her from his seat facing hers in the limo. "My son has done very well for himself. I was disappointed when he decided not to join me at Langston Plastics and he struck out on his own. But he's made us proud."

Jenny liked Wayne's smile, his kind brown eyes behind his wire-rimmed glasses. Father and son were very formal with each other but she sensed a real respect between them. Before she could respond to Wayne's comment, the driver stopped in the circular drive in front of the house. Christopher opened the door and helped her out.

They climbed the steps together, close but not touching. Wayne followed behind them. When the front door opened, Jenny saw a woman with blond hair arranged attractively around her face and guessed it was Christopher's mother. Her eyes were also brown like Christopher's, her facial features a soft version of his.

She reached out to Jenny. "I'm Christopher's mother, Marjorie. It's so good to have you home, dear. Are you tired from the trip?"

"A little," she answered.

The older woman tucked her arm into Jenny's and led her inside. "I asked Pauline to fix a light lunch. Would you prefer a tray in your room?"

Jenny gazed around the foyer, at the dark, hardwood floor, the *étagère* beside a curved staircase, the gilded mirror and sconces hanging beside a large closet with an ornately panelled door. "I'm not sure…"

"Maybe she needs to get her bearings," a deep voice said from the doorway to the living room.

Jenny's gaze met probing green eyes that tried to see through her.

Christopher came to her side. "This is my cousin, Luke. He stopped at the hospital but didn't visit because he didn't want to confuse you with another strange face. Are you up to lunch with everyone or would you rather be alone?"

Luke's gaze was challenging, almost a dare. Christopher's cousin. He knew her past with Christopher; she didn't. Her stomach was rolling but she'd never admit it. "Lunch would be great. I can rest later." She forced a smile.

Christopher took her hand. "The dining room's this way. Mother, if you'd tell Pauline we're ready?"

His gesture had been protective, but the impression of his fingers on her palm told her somewhere deep inside she remembered being loved by this man…or else she was mightily attracted to him.

As Pauline set luncheon plates before them, Jenny attempted to make adequate replies when someone questioned her. During lunch, for the most part, the conversation revolved around people and events she had no memory of. Everyone watched her closely as she picked at her crab salad, and she felt like a museum piece on display. Encroaching fatigue made lifting her fork a chore, and her ribs hurt when she took a deep breath.

When the housekeeper served dessert and set a fruit tart before her, Jenny said, "It looks delicious but if you don't mind, I'll save mine for later."

Pauline's straight dark-brown hair was no-nonsense short and layered around her face. She studied Jenny curiously. "Of course it's no problem, ma'am. You just let me know when you want it."

After excusing herself and retracing her steps to the foyer, Jenny stood at the foot of the stairway, realizing she had no idea of where she was going. More tired than she'd ever felt, she leaned on the carved oak newel post.

Suddenly Christopher was by her side. "Are you all right?"

Drawing on every ounce of energy left in her, she pulled herself up to her full five feet six inches and squared her shoulders. "I'm fine. Can you show me to my room?"

He took her chin in his palm. "You look as if you're ready to collapse." Without warning, he swung her into his arms.

"What are you doing? I can climb the steps on my own steam—"

Holding her tight against him, he cut her off. "You never used to be so argumentative. And unless you want a doctor out here this afternoon checking you over, I'd suggest you cooperate."

Uncomfortable all of a sudden with his first name, she felt she needed some propriety between them. "Look, Mr. Langston, I will not have you managing my health or my life. Just because I don't remember a few years doesn't make me an invalid."

"Lack of memory doesn't. But your accident might. Not an invalid, but a woman who needs to recuperate. And my name is Christopher, or has your short-term memory deserted you, too?"

Something in the way he asked alerted her to an undercurrent, perhaps a clue to the anger she sensed now and then. To maintain better balance, she'd instinctively hooked her arms around his neck and her face was entirely too close to his. She could smell his cologne and a more basic male scent that increased her pulse rate and caused a swirling sensation in her belly that had nothing to do with the lunch she'd eaten.

In spite of the excitement dancing through her, she asked, "Do you believe I *have* amnesia?"

He didn't answer her until he reached the upstairs hall. Then he carried her past a settee against the wall, to the second room on the left, and set her down. "The doctor says you don't remember. You told me you don't remember."

On her feet again without his hard body pressed against hers, she drew a deep breath despite the pain in her ribs and confronted the doubts she'd sensed in him ever since she'd awakened. "You didn't answer my question. I want to know why you think I'd fake not remembering our marriage."

After studying her with an intensity that almost made her back away, he said, "I can't answer that."

"Can't or won't?"

Shaking his head, he touched her cheek, tracing the side of her face with his thumb. "Ever since you woke up, you're different. You look the same. Your voice sounds the same. But you're different," he said again as if he was trying to make sure of it.

"I don't know what you mean," she said softly, entranced by the feel of his skin against hers.

"It means I thought I knew you but...I don't know if I know you now. You were always quiet. You never questioned me or my decisions."

Yes, she'd always been quiet and maybe a little reserved. But she'd also always known what she wanted and directed her own life. Had that changed when she'd met this man? Because of her love for him? Or something else?

"I don't know who or how I was with you. I truly don't remember."

As his gaze held hers, she stopped breathing. Every fiber of her being told her this was a most important moment in her life, though she didn't know why. Finally, he stepped away and opened the door. "This is our bedroom."

Jenny tore her eyes from Christopher's and crossed the threshold into the master suite. As formal as the rest of the house, it looked like a picture from a magazine with its cherry, four-poster canopied bed and long dresser with flowers arranged in a crystal vase in the center, a jewelry box to one side, a photograph of her and Christopher Langston on the other. A wedding photograph. The bedspread, canopy and chairs in the sitting area bloomed with mauve and blue roses complemented by blue stripes. Although the room was large, right now the king-sized bed seemed to take up most of the space, and the man beside her the rest.

One thought sped through Jenny's mind. They'd slept in this bed together. When she looked at him, she knew he was remembering things she couldn't. The turmoil on his face pierced her heart, and she wondered if he was thinking about what they'd lost or something else that caused him to doubt what she told him.

"It's a beautiful room," she said as fatigue overtook her again. She made her way to the bed and sat on the edge, just wanting to swing her feet up and sleep until morning.

Christopher crossed to her and towered over her. "Your closet is the one on the left. Your nightgowns and things like that are in the left side of the dresser. Would you like to change?"

She supposed he knew which nightgown was her favorite and which drawer it was in. Exploring on her own without him watching her would help her get acquainted with the room later. "No. I'll just rest like this for a while."

Gesturing to the dressing area and beyond, he explained, "There's a whirlpool tub in the bathroom."

"I had a shower this morning at the hospital."

"You used to like to soak in bubbles in there."

When she met his gaze, she asked, "With you?"

She thought his face flushed slightly before he said, "I'm not a great fan of bubbles."

His perusal made her feel self-conscious, and she brushed her hair from her forehead.

"You look pale," he said. "I'll let you get some rest. There's a button on the wall by the nightstand for the intercom. Pauline can hear it and will bring you whatever you need."

"Thank your mother and father and Luke for being here to welcome me, though I'm not sure that was Luke's reason for being here," she added, her intuition telling her that Luke might not believe she had amnesia, either.

"Luke and I are more than cousins. We're friends. He's been worried about you."

"And about you," she guessed.

"Probably." Changing the subject, he directed, "Lie back and I'll cover you." He lifted a mauve satin comforter from the quilt stand at the foot of the bed.

She thought about arguing, but his tone had been gentle. In an instant, she'd kicked off her shoes and lain back on the soft pillows. He shook the comforter across the bed and pulled it up to her waist.

With him standing there, she couldn't relax. She thought about him carrying her up the steps, his hot, hard body against hers. "Thank you."

"For what?" His voice was gruff.

"For bringing me here. For trying to understand."

"But I don't," he said so seriously she knew that he wasn't just talking about her amnesia. With a nod at the button, he reminded her, "Call if you need anything."

Then as if he didn't belong in the room, as if he didn't belong there with her, he left quickly, closing the door behind him.

Chapter Two

When Christopher came down the stairs, Luke was sitting on the third step from the bottom, his long jean-clad legs stretched out on the polished hardwood floor.

"I've never known you to pass up dessert," Christopher quipped as he sat beside his cousin.

"I eat fast. Your mother is telling your dad about a cruise to Greece she'd like to take in the fall. He's giving her all the reasons why he can't get away then."

A few silent moments stood between the two men. Finally Christopher asked, "Any discussion about Jenny?"

"I don't think they know what to say about Jenny. Or think. Your mother just keeps calling her 'that poor dear.' I'm not sure it fits."

"I think Jenny *does* have amnesia."

"She could be acting."

Christopher shook his head. "She's not that good an actress. If she were, she wouldn't have been so disconcerted and upset the past few months. No, since she awakened, she's the same as she was from the first moment I saw her and yet..."

"There's something extra thrown in," Luke decided.

"You've noticed."

"From the first time you two met, I think she was in awe of you—shy with you. Now, she treats you like anyone else. As if she's your equal. It's kind of weird."

"Her doctor told me that sometimes there are personality changes after head trauma—bursts of anger, impatience. I haven't noticed any of that. Just more spirit."

"Do you like that spirit?" his cousin probed.

"I'm not sure. It's a little unnerving."

"And you still want to know if she had an affair." Luke's voice was low and didn't carry farther than the bottom step.

"I can't look at her or touch her and not wonder," Christopher confessed, his sense of betrayal so strong sometimes he wanted to shove his fist through a wall.

"What if she never regains her memory?"

In other words, what if he never knew the truth? "I don't know, Luke. I don't know if I can ever forgive her. And now, I don't even know if she wants a marriage."

Pushing himself up from the step, Luke stood. "You need time to figure it all out. And you will. I'm going to hit the road. Got a hot date tonight."

Letting go of the situation for a moment, Christopher chuckled. "All your dates are hot."

"That's exactly what I want you to think," Luke returned with a smile. "I've got to keep my reputation intact."

Luke did have the reputation of being a ladies' man now, but Christopher knew the reasons. Luke had lost his wife three years ago. He'd tried to forget by working and acting as if he enjoyed going out with a different woman every weekend. But Christopher knew better and one day Luke would, too. "Someday, a woman might see beyond your reputation. It might happen when you least expect it—maybe when you trade in your suit for jeans." Every year Luke personally oversaw one of the projects his family's foundation's grants paid for by acting as general contractor on a job and pretending he was an ordinary guy.

"Women might like to size up construction workers, but looking for a life with one is another matter. Speaking of the salt of the earth, have you heard from Jud lately?"

"With everything that's been happening, I forgot to tell you. He's driving in from Tyler with a new horse for me in a week or so. Maybe we can all get together then."

"Sounds good."

Christopher stood to walk Luke to the door.

His hand on the knob, Luke said, "Call me if you need me."

Remembering the night he'd found Jenny's note, how he'd reached for the phone to call Luke out of a sense of powerlessness he'd never felt before, he nodded. "I will." Their summers on the Star Four had bonded the three of them as closely as brothers. They knew they could depend on each other.

But as Christopher closed the door on Luke, he realized only he could get at the truth of what had happened in his marriage. He was on his own as he felt he had been most of his life.

Evening shadows played in the corners of the bedroom when Jenny opened her eyes and reoriented herself to her surroundings. As she sat up, she slid her legs over the side of the bed. Then she stared hard at each piece of furniture, willing herself to find a flash of recognition. That didn't work so she went to the closet, opening it slowly as if it were Pandora's box. It was a walk-in closet with rods full of clothes lining both sides. In the back, shelves and drawers covered the wall from floor to ceiling.

Pushing one dress aside after another, she soon realized the clothes meant nothing, nor did the shoes on the racks under them or the hats on the shelf above them. When she turned, she saw a pale blue robe and nightgown hanging on a hook on the back of the door.

Why not have a bubble bath? Maybe she could soak away some of the soreness.

The bathroom was as elegantly appointed as every other room. Mauve candles stood on crystal holders, their scent wafting around the bathroom. But Jenny noticed the wicks were white. Picking up a brass box on the marble vanity, she found matches. On a whim, she lit the largest candle then filled the tub. She found a decorative bottle with bubble bath. After she poured some into the water, she slipped out of her clothes and into the tub that was large enough for two.

Don't follow *that* train of thought, she told herself.

The bubbles floated around her as she closed her eyes, breathing in the scent of the candles.

Suddenly the bathroom door opened and Christopher stood in the doorway.

Jenny instinctively slid down further into the bubbles. But she couldn't help staring at Christopher, and as she did, her heart started pounding and anxiety rippled through her. But as quickly as the flash of sensation overtook her, it passed.

"Jenny? What's wrong?"

"Nothing. I just... Nothing's wrong. But I wish you'd go back into the bedroom and close the door until I get out."

He looked highly chagrined and turned so that he was

looking at the wall rather than her. "I'm sorry. When I couldn't find you, I got worried. I'll wait in the bedroom."

As Christopher stepped out of the bathroom, Jenny took a deep breath. Had she remembered Christopher just for that moment? The sensation was so strange...as if she'd been in the tub before and he'd come walking in. But why the panic and anxiety? Maybe it wasn't a memory at all—just an illusion with the candle lit, steam swirling and a very sexy man finding her naked.

Confusion fought embarrassment as she dried off and quickly slipped into the nightgown and belted the soft, clingy robe tightly around her waist. The damp ends of her long hair whispered across her shoulders as she crossed to Christopher. He'd set a tray on the marble-topped table in the sitting area.

"Pauline sent up tea and cookies. You didn't eat much at lunch."

Had he noticed or had the housekeeper? "A cup of tea would be nice. I don't have much of an appetite."

"You've already lost weight," he said gruffly. "You shouldn't lose any more."

She wondered exactly how much of her he'd seen under the bubbles. Color heated her cheeks as she sat on the love seat to pour a cup of tea. He sat beside her, his thigh brushing hers. Her hands trembled, and she set the cup and saucer on the tray before the tea could spill.

"You have an appointment with Dr. Coswell tomorrow morning at nine," Christopher informed her. "I made it early because I have to get to work afterwards. I've been away too long."

"I could have made my own appointment. And I don't need you to take me like some baby-sitter." His tone made her defensive. He was acting as if the accident and its results were her fault.

His gaze held hers. "I want to take you. It's important for me to consult with your doctor."

She sensed that undercurrent again, a hundred and one things he wasn't saying. "You don't trust me, do you? You think I'd hide something from you. Why would I do that?"

He frowned but his tone was patient. "I need to talk to your doctor about your care, about what to expect, about her conclusions after she examines you."

"I could tell you all those things."

"Let's not argue about this, Jenny." Christopher's jaw set in a rigid line.

But she couldn't let it go. "Because you say we shouldn't? What kind of marriage did we have that we can't discuss a subject until it's finished?"

Obviously disconcerted, he didn't answer for a moment. Finally he said, "We didn't argue. Our conversations were—"

"Simply on the surface? With no substance?"

He looked at her as if she was as much of a stranger to him as he was to her. "I suppose it depends what you mean by substance," he answered cautiously.

She shifted on the sofa to face him, her robe slipping open over her knee. "Oh, Christopher. Things that are important to both of us...that touch us deeply...that we feel strongly about. Two people can't help but argue or disagree once in a while about those subjects."

Golden sparks flashed in his dark-brown eyes, sparks that seemed to touch her everywhere. His gaze followed the line of her hair falling across her breasts, then settled on her lips. "What do you feel strongly about, Jenny?"

The pull toward this man was so intense, she wanted to lean toward him and feel his arms around her again. But she answered his question instead. "I feel strongly about my photography, having a studio some day, making the world a better place where children can grow up safely with everything they need.''

"And what do *you* need?'' He asked the question as if it were the first time and he'd never asked before.

She shook her head. "I don't know. I feel so disoriented. Like someone's set me down on a strange planet where nothing's familiar. I guess most of all I need time to see if my memory will return, to figure out where I belong.''

Taking her hair in his hand, he let it slide through his fingers. "I didn't mean to barge in on you in the bathroom like that. I keep forgetting that in your mind, we're not married.''

She watched his fingers on her hair, imagining how they'd feel on other places. "You're a stranger to me, Christopher,'' she reminded herself as well as him.

"Maybe we should change that,'' he murmured, leaning closer, tempting her to find the passion they'd apparently once known.

But as Christopher's head bent, as his lips came closer to hers, the panic she'd experienced in the tub overtook her again.

Bracing her hands against his chest, she pushed away. "No. I can't.''

Christopher's features hardened. "Don't look so scared. I never forced myself on you in the past, and I never will.''

She *wasn't* scared. She intuitively knew he wouldn't hurt her. But the turmoil inside her kept her silent.

Christopher stood and went to the door. "I'll be in my office if you need anything.''

Before she could call out to him, to try and explain, he'd left the room and closed the door.

As her heart stopped pounding, she realized she didn't even know where his office was!

* * *

Choosing clothes from her closet was almost like going to a department store and picking something from the rack. There were so many dresses and slacks and sweaters. But she looked for something more casual and finally found a peach sweat suit in one of the drawers. She spotted sneakers and rummaged in a dresser drawer for socks. When she opened the top drawer out of curiosity, she saw a box of barrettes. She felt more together once she'd clipped her hair off her face, wrinkling her nose at the stitches, knowing the bruising would be gone in a few more days.

The upstairs of their house consisted of three guest bedrooms with their own bathrooms in addition to the master suite. She wondered if they'd had many overnight guests or else expected to have lots of children to fill the rooms. When she saw the room with her mother's bedroom set, she stopped and remembered the furniture where she'd last seen it, trying to push the grief away.

Jenny went from room to room downstairs, looking, touching, trying to remember. She noticed her mother's crystal and china in the dining room hutch, but nothing else evoked a memory or even a sensation as she'd experienced upstairs with Christopher. Tracing her steps back to the foyer, instead of going into the dining room, she explored a short hall, finding a powder room and a closed hardwood door beyond it. She rapped softly.

Christopher opened the door.

"I've been looking around. I hope you don't mind."

"Why should I mind? This is your home, too."

She peeked around him. "So this is your office?"

He motioned her inside, his gaze skimming her outfit.

"What?" she asked as he stared.

"I haven't seen you dressed like that in a long time."

"I wanted to be comfortable."

His smile was wry. "I think we'd both forgotten how to be comfortable."

"Why is that?"

"I'm usually in a suit all day. You always seemed to be dressed for luncheons or charity meetings."

She wandered to the bookshelves to check out the titles. "What about at night?"

"I get home late. You're usually in your nightgown or silk pajamas."

"We don't eat dinner together?"

"That was becoming more and more rare."

"I see." But she didn't really. Didn't they spend time together? Maybe on weekends. "You said you have stables. I thought I'd take a walk and look around."

"Are you sure you're up to it?"

"The nap helped. And I'm feeling restless. You don't have to come along. I just didn't want you to worry again."

After he glanced at the stack of computer printouts on his desk, he said, "I'll come with you and introduce you to Fred."

"And to the horses," she said with a smile.

As they strolled down the path from the kitchen to the stables, Christopher watched the last rays of sun shine on Jenny's hair. She looked so young in the sweats, with the barrette in her hair. So desirable. When he'd seen her naked in that tub...

He couldn't get the picture out of his head. About a month ago, he'd come home from work and found her there. She'd looked as if she'd been crying. But when he'd asked if something was wrong, she'd said she'd gotten soap in her eyes when she'd washed her hair. Then she'd invited him to bathe with her. But he'd told her he'd just stopped at home to explain that he had to pack a few things and fly to Boston. He'd be back the next day. She'd looked so...sad. But she'd smiled and wished him a good trip.

What if he'd stayed home that night? What if he'd gotten into the tub with her? Would she still have written him a note and left to go somewhere secret? To meet someone?

When he'd sat next to her in the bedroom earlier, he'd almost forgotten her note...her betrayal. But her pushing him away had brought it all back. The distance between them. His suspicions. Her amnesia.

He couldn't wait to see what happened with the horses. This was one way to find out once and for all if her amnesia was real.

As they walked, Jenny looked around as if she'd never seen any of it before—the manicured lawn, the stand of pines, the rose garden with its benches and fountain. He'd provided her with everything she could possibly want. Still, it hadn't been enough.

At the stable door, she didn't stop and wait for him to open it as she would have in the past. She flipped the wooden bar and opened the door herself. Once inside, Christopher called for Fred but received no answer.

"He's probably at the carriage house. C'mon. I'll introduce you to the horses myself."

Jenny followed him to the first stall where a huge bay whinnied at them. She stood a good foot away from the rungs of the stall, her hands behind her back. "I've never been around horses. But I've always thought they are the most beautiful animals."

Christopher remembered Jenny's first visit to his stable on one of their dates. She'd put up a brave front, pretending that going riding when she'd never done it before was not a big deal. But on the trail, the horse he'd chosen for her had gone from a walk to a trot to a canter when something spooked her, and Jenny had been frightened enough not to go riding again. At the beginning of their marriage, he'd tried to coax her into morning or evening rides with him, but she'd always refused.

Now she tentatively stepped closer to the bay that had caused her former fear and asked, "Can I pet her?"

In the past, he'd approached Jenny's introduction to horses and riding all wrong. If he'd realized how frightened she'd been, he would have done it differently. Fate had provided him with a second chance.

Going to a cupboard hanging above the feed barrels, he opened a container and took out a cube of sugar. "Carrots are better. But this is a treat. Give me your hand."

When she did, he laid the cube in her palm. "Her name is Wind Feather. Hold your hand out to her and let her take it from you. Her lips are soft and will tickle."

"She won't bite?"

He shook his head. "She wants the sugar, not your hand, though she might nuzzle you for more. Keep your palm flat."

Jenny stepped closer to the horse and held out her hand.

Wind Feather neighed softly, then lapped the sugar from her. Jenny laughed, a sound Christopher realized he hadn't heard for a long while.

"She likes to be scratched between her ears," he revealed, waiting to see what happened next.

Without hesitation, Jenny climbed up two of the stall's rungs. When Wind Feather didn't back away, she combed the black forelock with her fingers and rubbed between the horse's ears. "She's so pretty. If I stay, do you think you could teach me to ride?"

Her amnesia *was* real. Jenny, before the accident, wouldn't have gotten this close to Wind Feather, let alone thought about mounting her again. But his wife had just said something that made his stomach clench. "*If* you stay?"

She climbed down, her arm holding her ribs as she put her feet on the ground.

"You shouldn't be—"

"I'm fine, Christopher. Still sore, that's all. I'll heal."

Clasping her by the shoulders, he felt the sudden need to touch her, kiss her, hold her close. "I don't want you taking chances. I don't want you on some dark road again on a rainy night."

"If you tell me why I was there maybe I won't do it again."

"I don't *know* why you were there," he exploded, some of his anger impossible to contain.

"And you want me to stay with you so you can find out."

"I want you to stay with me because we were married for four years and you're my wife. You have nowhere else to go. Why would you want to leave?"

"Because I don't feel as if I belong here. Nothing's mine—"

"Everything is yours!" He grabbed her hand and pulled her to the door. "Do you see that rose garden? It wasn't there before you came. But you loved roses. So Fred planted them. We ordered the benches and the fountain. Every season, you tell Fred what flowers to grow and where to grow them."

"Did I decorate the house?"

Something told him she already knew but she wanted confirmation. "No. An interior decorator did after I bought it. Before we were married."

"And I didn't cook, did I?"

"Rarely. Pauline makes up the menus and leaves meals when she's off."

"Christopher, what did I *do?* How did I fill my days?"

He was beginning to realize how little time he'd spent at home. Or with Jenny. But his ego wouldn't let him admit it to her. "You've *always* wanted to make the world a better place. Tomorrow I'll show you your files where you organized all the details of the charities you worked with."

"Did I volunteer?"

"Mostly behind-the-scenes work. Mother does want to know... Well, I'll let her ask you."

"My life sounds so...so isolated."

He looked down at his wife who was struggling to understand the life she'd chosen. Would she choose it now? Would she choose him? "It might sound that way, but we have family, friends..."

"Women I had lunch with? Did we drop by each other's houses for coffee? Did I have that kind of friends?"

He was chagrined to admit he didn't know. "I don't know how you spent your days, Jenny. I was working."

Her gaze grew troubled, and she ran her hand through her hair away from her face. It was a gesture he was beginning to recognize that she used when she was trying to figure something out.

Turning away from the perfectly gardened lawn and grounds, she wandered back to Wind Feather, and this time without hesitation, stroked the horse's nose. "So...when my ribs heal, will you teach me to ride?"

It seemed she'd made some sort of decision, though he didn't know what it was. At least for the time being, she would stay. "I'll teach you to ride." And this time he'd do it slowly, without making a mistake. "My cousin Jud is bringing me a horse from Texas in a week or so. If I can convince him, I'd like him to stay a few days. If that's all right with you."

She cocked her head and studied him. "I don't mind. But why should you have to convince him?"

"The work on the Star Four keeps him tied up, and he can't get away for long. Uncle Thatcher had a serious heart attack in February, and Jud has basically taken over running the ranch and overseeing the training of the cutting horses."

"Do I know him well?"

"You know Luke better since he's closer. But you and Jud always got along if that's what you're asking me."

The anguish on her face at her lack of memories was as real as his suspicions that she'd been hiding something from him before her accident. It was so hard for him to separate the past and the present. "Jenny, I want to help you remember."

"I *need* to remember," she said, her eyes as vibrantly blue as he'd ever seen them.

Despite his anger and the sense of betrayal, he had so many deep feelings for this woman that had begun the moment he'd met her. She'd touched a place in him that had needed her softness, gentleness and sweetness. He still needed it. Maybe if he kissed her, her memories of him would return...

He slid his hand under her hair, and when she didn't back away, he took it as a sign of consent. Bending his head, he touched his lips to hers. All the longing, all the aching, all the praying that she'd live to come home again, drove him to thrust his tongue into her mouth and take the passion he wanted her to give back to him.

And she did give it back for a few inflammatory moments that had his heart pounding, his pulse racing, his body straining for union.

But then abruptly she tore away...away from his lips and out of his arms.

"Jenny..."

"You think I'm your wife. I don't remember *being* your wife. I can't just fall back into a role you want me to play."

"A role? Do you think that's what I want? I want our lives back!"

Her eyes glistened. "That might not be possible."

He shook his head, feeling as if his world had turned upside down. "I can't believe you don't remember any of it, that you don't *feel* anything."

"I didn't say I don't feel anything. I wanted you to kiss me," she admitted.

"Why? As an experiment? Out of curiosity? To see if I'd turn you on?" As soon as he said it, he knew he'd gone too far.

She turned from him and crossed to the stable door. With the sunset framing her, she said, "I can find my way back. If you decide you don't want to take me to Dr. Coswell's office, leave the address on the table in the foyer. I can call a cab."

Hating the idea of her walking away, he knew he had no choice but to let her go. They both needed some space.

He went to the tack room for a saddle. Maybe a ride would help him sort his thoughts. Kissing Jenny certainly hadn't.

When Jenny returned to the house, she stopped in the dining room and stared at her mother's crystal in the hutch. It was an old-fashioned pattern, etched into the glass. She opened the door and took out a goblet, needing to hold something familiar in her hands. This crystal had been in her mother's hutch for as far back as she could remember. Holding the goblet brought back memories of special meals in her childhood home, holiday celebrations, a time when her mother and father had been the most important people in her life.

Kissing Christopher had shaken her to her very core. There had been no hint of anxiety or panic as when he'd leaned close in her bedroom. At the stable, she'd felt such an intense attraction to him, like an unseen force drawing her closer and closer to an all-consuming flame. But she couldn't let it happen. She didn't know who he was. She didn't know who *she* was.

And now she was so tired again, unsettled and confused. The doctor had told her that her energy would return day by day. But the emotional upheaval was far more difficult than physically recovering from the accident. Reverently, she placed the goblet back on the shelf and closed the door.

When she entered her bedroom, she saw a suitcase and purse on her bed that hadn't been in her room before. One corner of the suitcase was smashed, and she wondered if she'd had it in the car with her. Eagerly, she opened it. But all she found were wrinkled clothes and a cosmetics case.

Still hopeful of triggering a memory, she opened the leather purse and dumped it on the bed. Lipstick, a pen, tissues and a wallet. Opening the wallet, she found her driver's license, credit cards and photographs. There was a picture of her with her mother and father taken years before. Her father had been fifteen years older than her mother, but he'd been a strong, vital man until he'd been diagnosed with cancer when she was in high school.

Pushing aside sad memories, she studied another picture—one of Christopher with Luke and another man in a cowboy hat. He must be Jud. And there was a photo of her and Christopher, posed, taken in the rose garden.

With a sigh, she absently checked the fold where bills should be kept. There were several. But a small slip of white paper between them caught her eye. It was folded.

When she opened it, she read—Marty 6/8. Who was Marty? Was 6/8 a date? It was written in her handwriting. She recognized that.

Why couldn't she remember?

Folding the paper again, she left it with the bills and stuffed the wallet and other things back into the purse. Then she crossed to the hall and went to the guest room where there was something else that was familiar—her mother's bedroom set. Suddenly she remembered what Christopher had said. *We kept many of your mother's things.* The closet seemed to beckon to her.

When she opened it, she found a treasure trove—her mother's jewelry boxes, books, a favorite dress and coat, and a cedar chest full of pictures and other memorabilia. As she sorted through the pictures, tears started to fall and she became tossed between happy memories and a sadness she'd never known.

Finally exhausted by the day and everything she'd had to absorb, she curled up on the bed with her mother's favorite silk scarf in her hands.

The work on Christopher's desk caused him more consternation than satisfaction as he entered data into the computer. It would help if he could concentrate on the numbers he typed in and not have to check the monitor two or three times after each one. At last, after midnight, he decided concentration was a lost cause and he might as well shut down the computer for the night.

When he reached the top step of the staircase, he saw the open door of the master suite and couldn't just walk by. But when he looked inside, he found it empty, the bed still made with the suitcase and Jenny's purse lying on top. If her purse was there, she couldn't have gone far. Certainly she wouldn't have left this time of night. Not unless…

He checked her bathroom. Not finding her, he was about to search downstairs when he saw the door to one of the guest bedrooms ajar. When he pushed it open, he saw Jenny curled on the bed, her mother's scarf under her cheek. The closet door stood open, and he realized she'd been looking through her mother's things. His heart ached for her.

As he stood watching her, she murmured in her sleep. Tossing from one side to the other, she said, "No. No. Don't leave. No."

Hurrying to her, he sat beside her on the bed. "Jenny. Wake up. Jenny."

As soon as she heard his voice, her eyes opened. It took her a moment to focus on him and her surroundings. "I had a dream."

"What was it?"

She sat up. "My mother was walking down this long tunnel away from me. And there was this shadow of a man…"

"Your father? Me?"

"I…don't know. It was just a shadow. He was tall but…" She shook her head.

"Was it a dream or a memory?"

"A dream."

She seemed sure, but he wondered if memories were trying to surface. And the man…he had to face the fact it could be her lover. She was unaware right now of that possibility, but he wasn't.

"If you don't mind, I'm going to sleep in here tonight," she murmured.

"Why should I mind?" he asked gruffly as he stood. "You sleep where you feel most comfortable. I'll see you in the morning."

Before he could leave, she clasped his arm. "Christopher, I kissed you earlier because I wanted to kiss you. I'm very attracted to you. But right now, that attraction is as confusing as not remembering.''

Her honesty tempted him to sit beside her, take her in his arms, and make love to her until she forgot her confusion. But he knew that wouldn't help her remember or solve the mystery of her whereabouts before her accident.

When he didn't respond immediately, she released his arm. But before he moved away, he said, ''I'll see you at breakfast and I'll take you to the doctor's.'' At the door, he stopped. ''I hope the rest of your dreams are pleasant ones. I'm next door if you need me.''

As he went to his room, he realized he wanted her to need him, but he didn't want to need her.

And he did.

Chapter Three

Jenny's breakfast with Christopher was strained, and when he drove her to her appointment with Dr. Coswell, their conversation didn't flow any easier. In the waiting room, he checked his watch at least three times. He looked so handsome this morning in a navy suit, white shirt, and red and navy patterned tie. But he also seemed more distant. Ever since the kiss. Ever since she'd pushed him away.

It wasn't long until the nurse showed them to an office where a middle-aged woman sat behind her desk. Her brown hair was streaked with gray and her eyes were kind. She motioned to the two chairs. "I thought we'd talk before I examine you." Standing, she shook both their hands. "I'm Mary Coswell. I spoke with Dr. Bartlett in Binghamton and he faxed me your records. Mr. Langston, I know your wife is the patient, but I'm glad to see you here. With the type of trauma Jenny has experienced, she'll need your support."

Jenny glanced at Christopher. His expression revealed

nothing about his thoughts on the subject until he said, "I want to help my wife remember."

The doctor nodded. "I'm sure you do. But I hope both of you are aware that Jenny might never regain her memory."

Jenny leaned forward in her chair. "When will I know? How will I know?"

Dr. Coswell shifted toward her. "If you start having flashbacks, mental pictures, that's a very positive sign. But you have to understand there are no norms here. Each person is different. I know what I'm telling you doesn't help your sense of frustration that you've lost part of your life, but I'd like you to keep in mind how fortunate you are. You survived the accident. You've lost five years. Some of my head trauma patients lose all memory, along with their ability to talk and walk."

If Jenny had been feeling sorry for herself the past few days, Dr. Coswell's words put her accident in perspective. She was blessed to be alive, to be whole in most senses of the word. From this moment on, she'd do her best to build on what she knew, what she had, what she could do. Because forward was the only direction to go.

Her gaze met Christopher's. He was holding something back from her, she was sure of it. There were questions and doubts in his eyes she couldn't begin to address because she didn't know what put them there. She vowed to herself she'd find out exactly what kind of marriage they'd had whether she regained her memory or not.

After Dr. Coswell examined her and removed her stitches, the physician handed her two of her business cards. When Jenny met Christopher in the waiting room, she gave one to him. "Dr. Coswell said if you have any questions or if something happens we don't understand, we should call her."

He fingered the card. "Did you tell her about your dream?"

"I didn't think there was anything to tell. It was just a dream."

"When is your next appointment?" he asked in an even tone. Yet she sensed the edge he was trying to cover.

"In two weeks. She thinks my ribs will be healed by then. Maybe she'll give me the okay to go riding."

He studied her closely. "You still want to?"

"Sure. I'm going to spend time with Wind Feather every day so she gets used to me. Then when I want to ride her, we'll be friends."

The tense lines around Christopher's eyes seemed to relax, and he smiled. "Good plan."

"And I have another. It's silly for you to drive me home then drive back in to your office. I'll just take a taxi."

"Jenny…"

"I'm fully capable of getting in a cab and letting someone chauffeur me. You can't keep treating me as if I'll break."

He didn't look pleased with her decision, but after glancing at his watch once again, he gave in. "All right. But I'll put you in the cab myself."

She sighed. Whoever she was in their marriage before, she'd have to show Christopher Langston she didn't need his constant care and protection now. She was going to move forward, with or without his approval.

Tuesday morning, Jenny spent time in the stables with Wind Feather then explored the grounds and enjoyed the sunny April weather, the scent of fresh-mown grass, the joy of being outside. She had to admit she missed Christopher. He was her anchor in an unfamiliar world. But she hadn't seen him since she'd said goodbye and gotten into the cab yesterday. Last evening Pauline had given her the message that he wouldn't be home until late. Jenny had heard his car in the drive at three a.m. He'd already left this morning before she was up. She was beginning to suspect that this was the type of life they'd led. Unless he was staying away on purpose. Unless he was so far behind from his time by her bedside that he had no choice but to work late.

After lunch, she rested for a while and then found Pauline and asked her if she knew where she kept her camera equipment. She'd searched every nook and cranny on the first and second floors and hadn't found even one camera.

Pauline looked surprised when Jenny asked, but smiled and beckoned her to follow. They descended a stairway from the kitchen and Jenny found another suite of rooms.

"You spent a lot of time down here, ma'am," Pauline said as she led Jenny into a large open area with a big-screen television, a long off-white sofa and plush teal carpeting. A Ping-Pong table stood in one corner, but it didn't look as if it had seen much use.

The housekeeper rapped on a closed door. "That was your darkroom." She opened the closet beside it. All Jenny's photographic equipment was stacked on the shelves. But it looked as if it had been stored carefully and not touched for a while.

"When did I stop taking photographs?" she asked.

"About two years ago."

"Do you know why?"

"You never confided in me, ma'am. But I suspect it was because you became more and more involved in your charity work. This was your office."

Pauline opened a door that led into a room with a computer and printer situated on a hutch unit with shelves and a desk. A file cabinet standing against the wall beside a stereo system must have been the one Christopher had referred to.

The office had been decorated in off-white with abstract paintings on the walls in taupe and brown. "Didn't I decorate this, either?" Jenny blurted out before she thought better of it.

"No, ma'am. You always called Mr. Langston's decorator and she took care of problems like that."

"This room needs some color, and those paintings have to go."

"They're originals, ma'am."

Jenny wrinkled her nose. "Original 'what' is what I'd like to know."

Pauline laughed. "I imagine they spoke to the decorator."

Jenny smiled at Pauline's wry tone. "I imagine they did, but they don't speak to me. And, Pauline, call me Jenny please."

"All right, ma...Jenny. Will you be staying down here?"

"For a while."

"There's an intercom," the housekeeper said, pointing to it. "Just call if you need anything."

Pauline left Jenny in her office, but she didn't stay there long. Instead, she went to the closet and began checking her cameras. She found a thirty-five millimeter she'd used in college and searched the closet for film. There was none there. Or in the darkroom. Suddenly, she itched to take some pictures. She'd go to WestFarms Mall for the supplies she needed.

After she changed and called a cab, she told Pauline she was going shopping. The housekeeper offered to get Fred so he could drive her, but Jenny explained she'd already called a taxi. She was looking forward to being on her own for a while.

Three hours later Jenny glanced at her watch as the cab driver took her home. Her trip had taken her a little longer than she'd planned. She felt the shorter hair on the nape of her neck and smiled. After she'd stocked up on film and ordered supplies for the darkroom, she'd spotted the hair salon and on impulse gone inside. Finding she didn't need an appointment, she'd waited until the next stylist was free. She felt lighter without all that hair, different, more ready for a new life. Stopping at a store in the same mall, she'd selected throw pillows in greens and blues and sunset pink for the television area and two area rugs in the same colors for her office. She would take down the abstracts and work on the walls next.

As the cab pulled into the circular drive, she saw Christopher's sedan parked at the front entrance. Paying the cabbie from the bills in her purse, she thanked him and climbed out, clutching the bag of film. No sooner had she climbed the steps, realizing how her excursion had again drained her energy, when the front door opened and Christopher stood there, his white shirtsleeves rolled to his elbows, a fierce scowl on his face.

"Where have you been?" he demanded before she could even smile and say hello.

"At the mall."

As if he'd just noticed, he bellowed, "And what the hell have you done to your hair?"

She fluffed the bangs, then the shorter back with her free hand. "Don't you like it?"

His jaw dropped in disbelief that she'd asked.

"Christopher, what's the problem?"

His stance was rigid, the nerve in his jaw working. "The

problem is that I called to see how you were, and Pauline had no idea where you'd gone.''

"I told her I was going shopping. I'm an adult so don't treat me like a runaway teenager.''

He pointed to the small bag. "That took you three hours?''

"Of course not! I had the other purchases sent because I didn't want to lug them.''

"And what was so important that you couldn't wait for Fred to take you or me to drive you?''

She didn't know exactly what Christopher's problem was, but she decided he was upset because he was concerned about something more than her health. "I felt like going out, on my own. I'm over eighteen and this is a free country, so do you want to tell me what I did that's so terribly wrong?''

"I was worried!''

"You were worried?'' she flung back. "Is that why you didn't come home until three a.m.? Why you left before breakfast? Why you didn't bother to leave a note whether or not you'd be home for dinner? I don't think *worried* is the right word to use. And if this constant surveillance is your idea of marriage, then it's no wonder neither of us knows why I was on a dark road at night outside of Binghamton!''

At Christopher's stunned expression, she realized she mustn't have lost her temper very much since she'd known him. Matter of fact, he had said they hadn't argued. Well, she wasn't arguing now. She was stating facts.

Pushing the front door wide open, she went inside and up the stairs to her room.

Jenny's words had hit Christopher like a physical blow. She had never confronted him that way before! But then he had never questioned her like today, either. He *had* been worried about her.

Worried her memory had returned and she'd run into the arms of another man?

He swore, raked his hand through his hair, and gazed out over the lush green lawn, the rows of garden waiting for perennials to come up, the drive that led to the main road. Jenny had never complained about his late hours. And it had been a very long time since she'd asked him what time he'd be home. She'd always been here waiting—in bed, ready to welcome him with her body, or in her office where she developed new ideas to raise money and the ways to execute them.

But now...

Now he was beginning to realize how much he'd left her alone.

He hadn't had to apologize often in his life. But he realized if he didn't apologize to her now, she might pack up her bags and leave! In fact, she might be packing at this moment...

Closing the door with a slam, he took the steps two at a time. The door to her room was slightly ajar and he pushed it open, expecting to see an open suitcase on the bed. But instead, he found Jenny in the middle of the spread, loading film into a camera.

When she looked up, he breathed a sigh of relief and said, "I guess I should have knocked."

She shrugged. "I left the door open."

"Hoping I'd come up?"

Sliding to the edge of the bed, she laid the camera aside. "I don't know what I hoped. Do you have any idea of how...disoriented I feel?"

He sat on the bed beside her. "No, I probably don't."

When she tilted her chin up to meet his gaze, her shorter hair brushed her cheek. "Thank you for being honest."

Today nothing but honesty shone in *her* eyes. She handled the disorientation well and faced her present condition with a courage he didn't know if he could manage. Yet he couldn't help but remember shadows in her eyes and on her face the few months before her accident rather than the sincerity he saw now.

Wanting to touch her, to kiss her, to lay her back on the bed and make love to her until only he was her world, he knew they had a long way to go before truly becoming husband and wife again. At least his head knew it, even though his body had ideas of its own.

His head guided him now. "I overreacted when you came home. I'm sorry."

"You treated me as though I'm not supposed to make a move without your authorization. I can't live like that."

He heard the certainty and marveled at this Jenny's outspoken manner and wondered why the old Jenny had become so quiet. "I know you can't. And our marriage wasn't that way. Jenny, you said you're disoriented. I'm a little off-kilter myself. After your accident, I didn't know if you were going to live or die or ever function normally again. You've only been out of the hospital three days and I *am* worried about you."

She covered his hand so naturally with hers that the arousing sensation of her skin on his was eclipsed by the sheer satisfaction that she *wanted* to touch him, especially after his third degree.

"I'm fine, Christopher. Really. My ribs feel better every day. I still get tired after expending energy, but that's getting better, too. So you don't have to worry about me."

Wanting her to keep her hand on his, wanting to keep her talking he asked, "So what did you buy?"

"Film and batteries. Supplies for the darkroom. I want to start shooting and developing again. Then I bought a few things for my office. I charged everything. I hope that's okay."

"You don't have to ask me to buy what you want. Your checkbook is in your desk downstairs. Pauline said you found the files. I meant to take you down there, but..."

"Your work had backed up," she guessed.

He'd never felt guilty about the hours he worked. Why did he now? "My business doesn't just involve research on American companies but on foreign ones also. I have to make many of the international calls at night."

"What exactly do you do?"

"I invest other people's money as well as my own."

"And you must do it very well."

There was curiosity in her voice. He'd never talked to Jenny very much about his work, thinking she'd be bored. "I had a lot of time on my hands as a kid. I was a fast learner. So my parents sent me to an elite boarding school where they thought I'd be challenged. I hated it, the I'm-better-than-everyone-else attitude of the students there. I hated being away from everything familiar...from Luke who was more like a brother than a cousin. Anyway, I couldn't seem to connect to the other kids at school like I did with Luke and Jud in the summers, so when I wasn't studying or playing soccer, I analyzed the stock market."

Jenny smiled. "As a pastime."

"Yep. It started as a hobby, but it fascinated me. Luke, Jud and I got paid for the summers we worked on my uncle's ranch. The year I was fourteen I convinced them to trust me with their money. I went to my father with my ideas and he followed them and invested it for me."

"And it grew?"

He laughed. "It sure did. Every year after that, Luke and Jud not only handed me their salary, but their savings, too."

She was staring at him still with a hint of a smile.

"What?" he asked, feeling self-conscious.

"I'm trying to imagine you in a cowboy hat and boots."

"And?"

Suddenly she averted her eyes and took her hand from his. He could have dropped the whole discussion, but he wanted to know exactly what was in Jenny's head. Hooking his finger under her chin, he turned her toward him. Her cheeks were flushed.

"Tell me."

Her gaze passed over his face. "I think you'd make one very sexy cowboy."

She'd said it so simply, with a shyness that aroused him as fast as her touch could, that even his head couldn't keep him from curving his arm around her and lacing his fingers into her hair. With his blood pounding hard and fast, his desire greater for her than he ever imagined, he found her lips with an abiding hunger that wouldn't let go.

When Jenny's hand reached up to his shoulder, he prayed she wouldn't push him away. Instead of resisting him, she slid her hand up his neck with such an exquisite sense of discovery that Christopher's groan came from deep inside his soul. He thrust his tongue into her mouth and laid her back on the bed, not stopping to think about the consequences. He swept her mouth and pressed his palm to her breast.

The phone beside the bed rang. Then it rang again and again...

For whatever reason, Pauline wasn't picking up. When he'd called the housekeeper from work and discovered Jenny had left, he'd postponed a meeting, telling his mutual fund managers to call him if they needed him.

Breaking away from Jenny, his breathing ragged, he snatched up the receiver. "Langston."

There was a full moment of consideration before the line went dead.

He swore, his pulse pounding for a different reason than it had a minute before.

Jenny's new hairdo was mussed, her lips rosy from his kiss. "What's wrong?"

Closing his eyes for a second against the turmoil raging inside him, he tried to get a grip on his emotions. Another hang-up call. Someone had been on the end of that line. He was sure of it.

Jenny's lover?

He didn't know how to separate the present from the past, any more than he could separate the woman on the bed from his wife before her accident. "It must have been the wrong number," he said, his voice gruff with anger and regret and the need to know who was calling his wife.

"Christopher…"

No way did he want to talk about that kiss or his desire or what almost happened between them. "I'd better check with Pauline to see why she didn't pick up. Then I have to go back to the office. I'll be working late again tonight. I don't know what time I'll be home."

"You don't have to go into your office to get away from me."

"I'm not…" He snapped his mouth shut. There was no point lying to her or to himself. "I have some things to sort out. It's easier when I'm not here."

"Because I am," she said, her face telling him that she was hopeful he might deny it.

But he couldn't. "You needed to get out this afternoon. I need to get out now." He stood, straightened his tie and crossed to the door.

When he turned to look at her, her eyes were big and blue and uncertain.

"I don't have any answers, Jenny. Not yet. I'll see you tomorrow." As he closed the door behind him, he couldn't forget the look in her eyes. He couldn't forget his body pressing against hers. He couldn't forget that she might have been unfaithful.

Two hours later, Christopher sat at his desk in his office suite, expecting a return call and unable to concentrate. When the phone rang, he snatched it up, realizing this was probably the first time in his life he was going to ask for advice. But that hang-up incident at home had pushed him into a corner and made him face reality.

"Langston," he answered.

"Mr. Langston, it's Dr. Coswell."

"You said to call if I have any questions. I need to know how to handle something."

"Go ahead."

Picking up his pen, he clicked it open and shut. "Will what I say to you be confidential?"

"Mr. Langston, I don't discuss my patients with anyone without their permission."

"No, I mean what *I* say to you."

"I extend the same confidentiality to my patient's family. Now, if you want me to keep something from Jenny, that's another matter."

He went ahead anyway because he needed the doctor's opinion. "Something was pulling my marriage apart before Jenny's accident, and I believe she was having an affair. I don't know why she was on that road near Binghamton or where she was going. I'd like to deal with all of this out in the open, but if she doesn't remember any of it, we can't."

"*If* she doesn't remember?"

He laid the pen on the blotter. "She doesn't remember. At least not yet."

"This is affecting your relationship."

"As much as her amnesia is."

"And you want to know if you should tell her your suspicions."

"Yes."

There was silence for a few moments. "Is she having any flashbacks or fragments of memories?"

"If she is, she hasn't told me."

"Do you want to do what's best for you or what's best for Jenny?"

On his desk sat a photograph of him and Jenny on their honeymoon in Hawaii. "I'll do what's best for Jenny."

"Then in my opinion, it's best if she remembers naturally, without any traumatic revelations. She hasn't even been out of the hospital a week, Mr. Langston. When she acclimates herself to her surroundings again, the memories could start coming back. Give her time to remember on her own."

"How much time? Two months? Six months?"

"I don't know. I realize that's not what you want to hear. But with head trauma, I can't give you exact answers."

"So there's nothing I can do."

"You can support her. You can start building a new relationship with her. You can be patient and wait."

When Christopher hung up the phone, he realized he hadn't gotten the advice he wanted, but Dr. Coswell had given him the answer to his question. He couldn't share his suspicions with Jenny.

He'd have to live with his doubts and hope his marriage could survive.

* * *

Wind Feather cantered across the grass late Friday morning, head up high, tail flying. Jenny shot the beauty in motion, the twitch of the mare's ear, the lift of her nostril—click after click as she tried to distract herself from thinking about Christopher and her growing feelings for him. She'd figured out something about him the past few days. When he didn't know how to deal with her feelings or his, he put distance between them. Had he always done that?

Moving to another stretch of fence, she turned the camera for another perspective, a different angle. Suddenly, the hairs on the back of her neck prickled. She lowered her camera, knowing Christopher was approaching. Wondering why he was home before lunch when he'd left before breakfast, she turned to face him.

When his gaze passed over her, her jeans and knit top might as well have been transparent because she swore he could see through them. At least that's the way his intense regard made her feel. "What are you doing home? Is something wrong?"

"I'm not checking up on you if that's what you're wondering," he answered brusquely. "I left some papers here that I need at the office. And I wanted to discuss something with you."

"Here I am," she said with a smile that only made him frown.

"Mother called. She's having a dinner party tonight and wondered if we'd like to come. I didn't know if you were up to it."

"Sure, I am. Who will be there?"

"Some friends of my parents, Luke and his parents. You knew them all. That's why I wasn't sure you'd want to go."

His face gave no hint as to what he was thinking, and

she didn't understand his comment. "Would you rather I hide away?"

"Of course not. I was just thinking of you and the questions you might have to field…"

"*We* might have to field, don't you mean? I was in an accident. I have no memory of our marriage. I have nothing to be ashamed of and neither do you."

Christopher's brows drew together. "Did you ever stop to think that questions might be awkward for me since our marriage is the only aspect of your life you *don't* remember?"

So that's what was bothering him. "Oh, Christopher. I'm sorry I wasn't thinking. We don't have to go."

He jammed his hands into his trouser pockets. "I don't need your sympathy. And we're not going to hide. I just want you to realize what we're both facing."

Unable to keep herself from reaching out to him, she clasped his arm. "It's not sympathy. It's understanding. And I don't know why I can't remember our marriage any more than you do. Unless you know something you're not telling me," she added softly.

The turmoil in his eyes flashed for only a moment. Then their brown depths were shuttered again. "I called Dr. Coswell the other day because I was concerned about you. She reiterated what she told us before. Injury from head trauma is unpredictable."

"You called her because you were concerned about me?"

"Why are you so surprised? I care about you, Jenny."

She couldn't keep from speaking her thoughts. "Then come home at night so we can get to know each other again." She'd waited up the last three nights, hoping. But she'd fallen asleep before he'd come in every night.

When he took his hand from his pocket, she thought he

was going to pull away from her grasp. But he didn't. He simply looked down at her and asked, "Is that what you want?"

"Yes." There was an amazing current that vibrated between them. But she couldn't just give in to the sparks. She had to know where they came from. Releasing his arm, she wondered if she had always wanted to touch him like she wanted to touch him now.

"I'll be home by six tonight to get dressed. Mother expects us at seven."

"What should I wear?"

He smiled and looked her over. "Personally, I like the jeans. Where'd you find them?"

Apparently she'd dressed in casually elegant clothes even at home. "In the bottom of a drawer. But I don't think they're appropriate for a dinner party."

"Just look in your closet. You'll know what to wear. You have excellent taste. By the way, the things you bought on Tuesday arrived. They're in the foyer."

"Want to see what I bought?" she asked with a grin. When he checked his watch, she said, "Never mind. I didn't buy anything earth-shattering."

"So show me anyway. Where do you want the packages?"

"Downstairs. But if you need to get back..."

"I have fifteen minutes. C'mon. Let's go to the house and you can show me what you bought."

Jenny's silence as they walked toward the back of the house made Christopher regret his time limit. She probably thought he was trying to humor her. Guarding his reactions to her was costing him. But he had to watch what he said...what he did...what he felt.

In the foyer, Christopher lifted two giant bags and carried them downstairs, wondering what was inside. Jenny had piqued his curiosity. She seemed excited about what she'd bought. She'd picked up a third, smaller bag and started unwrapping it as they went down the steps.

He watched as she tore open the packages, scattering the colorful pillows on the sofa. Before he realized what she was doing, she'd taken one of the rugs to her office. She winced when she lifted it, and he realized she was healing but she wasn't healed.

Taking it from her hands, he asked, "Where do you want it?"

"In front of the file cabinet. And I'd like the other one in the doorway."

After he'd spread them where she'd directed, he looked into the sitting area, then around her office. "You've added life down here."

With a smile, she said, "Now all I have to do is take those dreadful paintings off the wall. I thought I'd stop at Seneft's Gallery the next time I'm out and find something to replace them."

"What do you have in mind?"

"I'm not sure. But I'd like to pick up the colors in the rugs."

"You have some framed photographs in storage on the third floor."

"Really?" She looked like a child who'd just been handed a much wanted Christmas gift.

"Really. Would you like me to carry them down here for you?"

"Maybe Fred can do it. I know you have to get back."

At that instant he realized he didn't want to give the job to Fred...because he wanted to see her face when she first glimpsed the photographs she'd taken. "Do you mind waiting until tonight when we get home? I'd like to be here when you see them again."

"In case they bring back memories?"

Caught up in the moment, he'd forgotten about their circumstances. But he couldn't forget, and her reason was more substantial than his. "Yes. I think it would be better if we look at them together." Protecting himself again, he suggested, "Have Pauline get rid of the debris. I'll try to be on time tonight."

"Christopher?"

He stopped in the doorway.

"I'm really looking forward to tonight."

To being with him? Or to going to a party?

He didn't ask. He just nodded and left her in her office, thinking how pretty she looked and how much he wanted her.

Chapter Four

Rushing down the stairs, Christopher stopped short three steps from the bottom when he saw Jenny taking an off-white, light coat from the closet.

When she looked up, he was staring.

"I don't remember that dress," he said, his voice low and gruff.

"That's my line," she said with a smile that was supposed to put the evening on a good footing. She'd found the ice-blue silky sheath at the back of her closet, tags still attached.

"Turn around," he ordered as he came down the last two steps.

Tossing her coat over her arm, she spun in a circle. The halter top was sedate in the front but in the back revealed a circle of skin below her shoulder blades.

"You've never worn a dress like this before," he said as his finger traced the circle on her back.

His touch sent a shiver through her that was intoxicating

and arousing, as if her body knew what would happen next even if she didn't. "Maybe I bought it on a whim."

"Or maybe you bought it for a definite purpose." His voice had gone cold and before she could ask what he meant, he said, "Let's go or we'll be late."

One moment she felt as if he was attracted to her, the next as if he didn't want to touch her. Why would wearing a brand-new dress cause such a reaction?

Christopher's parents lived only a few miles away. He switched on the compact disc player and was giving off plenty of signals that he didn't want to talk. So much for getting the evening off to a good start, she thought.

Although a maid answered the door to the two-story colonial with its tall white pillars, Marjorie Langston met them in the parlor. She took Jenny's hand. "I'm so glad you came. How are you feeling? You look wonderful. Your hair is extremely attractive that way."

Jenny could feel a genuine warmth from Christopher's mother. "I'm feeling good. And so glad you invited us. But you'll have to introduce me to everyone."

"They understand about your accident. I told them all to pretend they're meeting you for the first time. Come along into the living room for hors d'oeuvres."

Christopher stayed beside her as his mother swept them into the midst of her party. Luke approached them first. In spite of herself Jenny was glad to see a familiar face. But when his gaze skimmed over her new hairdo and her dress, his brow arched at Christopher as if to say something only the two men would understand. For some reason, she wasn't sure yet whether Luke was a friend or foe. Yet he acted perfectly friendly when he introduced her to his parents. His mother and Marjorie were sisters. The Hobarts were as kind to her as Christopher's parents, and she soon relaxed when she found they were simply treating her like a new acquaintance rather than an oddity.

At dinner, Jenny found herself seated between Christopher and Marjorie with the Hobarts across from her. She felt protected, although the other four couples Marjorie had invited had been very pleasant. Still, she felt them watching her curiously now and then.

Christopher's arm brushed hers as he reached for his water goblet. Her gaze locked to his for a moment that seemed to stretch into hours. She couldn't read his thoughts but there was something he seemed to be searching for. She wished she knew what it was.

When Marjorie addressed her, she broke eye contact with him, wishing she could find out more about her marriage.

"Jenny, it might be too soon, but I have to know where you stand on a project you were working on," Marjorie began.

"I found the files I kept but I haven't had a chance to go through them yet."

"This involves a commitment. You agreed to chair an auction to raise money for an endowment we're donating to the hospital to help children who have no insurance coverage. I need to know if you still want to do it."

"What's involved?"

"You organized and delegated mostly, setting up the committee. Donations for the auction are coming in now, and we're storing them in one of our garages. You were also going to act as master of ceremonies for the auction because no one else wanted to do it."

"I need something to occupy me. This sounds like something I could delve into right away. *If* you can fill me in on everything I need to know."

Marjorie's smile was wide. "Of course I can, dear. Why don't we set up a meeting for next week. We have a few weeks until the night of the auction. You know you don't have to make a decision about this tonight if you'd like to think about it first."

"No, I don't need to think about it. It's exactly what I need."

Christopher leaned toward her, and his breath whispered across her cheek as he asked, "Do you have any idea of what you're getting yourself into?"

When she turned her head, her lips were a breath from his. "I want to do this, Christopher. I have the time. I can't just sit around the house, hoping I'll remember what my life used to be."

She thought she saw admiration flicker in his eyes, but then he leaned back and looked away.

After dinner Jenny excused herself to touch up her lipstick. Finished, she was about to turn the lock on the louvered powder-room door to exit when she heard her name mentioned. Telling herself she shouldn't eavesdrop, she did anyway.

"It's strange she was in Binghamton but no one knows why. Or if they do, they aren't saying."

"Marjorie won't talk about it at all. Do you think maybe she'd been drinking when she went off the road and that's why they're so hush-hush?"

Jenny froze. *Drinking?*

She'd never gotten into the party scene at college like some of the other students had. Sure, she had a glass of wine with friends now and then...

Is this why Christopher kept tabs on her? Had she developed a dependency on alcohol during their marriage? Was that the problem between them?

She had to know.

Purposefully, she unlocked the door with a loud click so the women outside would know she was exiting. When she opened the door, she gave them a forced smile and went to search for her husband.

She found the men in the library, a room with two walls of built-in bookshelves, a massive maple desk, leather sofa and chairs. Christopher was talking with two men who were smoking cigars. Ignoring the curious gazes of the men because she was audaciously entering their domain, she said to Christopher, "I'm sorry to interrupt, but I need to talk with you."

He was silent for a moment, and a little voice said, *He's going to tell you he's too busy.* The thought was an impression. Or was it an echo of a time before? Before she could decide, he nodded to the men and excused himself. Taking her by the elbow, he led her down a short hall to a glassed-in room with bright yellow-and-white striped wicker furnishings.

After he followed her inside, he asked, "What's wrong?"

She hadn't said anything was wrong, but he seemed very good at reading her. "Did I drive my car off the road because I was drunk?"

"Jenny!"

"Did I?"

"No. Of course not. Why did you even ask?"

"Because I heard two of your mother's friends talking about me, and they posed the possibility since none of you will discuss the accident."

"They're gossips, Jenny, even if they are Mother's friends. They think they have to know everything about everyone. My parents are more private than that."

"But it makes sense. If I developed a problem while we were married, that's why you're so distant most of the time, why you won't tell me about our marriage—"

Suddenly he was holding her by her shoulders. "Stop it.

You do *not* have a drinking problem. If you don't believe me, you can check your medical records. After an accident like yours, they check the blood alcohol level. You had *not* been drinking.''

Tears pricked in her eyes from the relief of at least knowing that much.

''And as far as our marriage, I'm following Dr. Coswell's suggestion. She feels you need to remember on your own.''

His hands on her shoulders were firm, and she longed to feel them on her bare skin. The longing came from more than surface attraction. It came from a place deep inside. ''And the distance?'' Her question was almost a whisper.

Releasing her, he stepped away. ''We're in an awkward situation. There's going to be distance.''

''But I feel as if you're angry with me for some reason. And if you won't tell me—''

''Isn't it enough that you turned our lives upside down with your accident? That before your accident, I had a wife, and now I don't?''

''I'm still your wife,'' she said softly.

''You've banished every memory of our marriage, and I'm sleeping in the guest room!''

''I asked you for some time...''

He slashed his arm through the air. ''Fine. Take all the time you need. But then don't ask me why there's distance between us.'' With that, he strode from the room.

Her knees shaky, Jenny sat on the striped love seat, struggling to hold back tears. She had to compose herself before she could face the party again. She had to figure out exactly what was best for her and Christopher and do it.

When she heard footsteps, she hoped Christopher was coming back so they could...

But as she looked up, she saw Luke.

He came in and stood over her, his expression serious. "Christopher looks as if he'd like to wrestle the first grizzly that crosses his path. Are you all right?"

Taking a deep breath, she said, "I don't know, Luke. Will you tell me about my marriage? Will you tell me if something was wrong?"

As tall as Christopher, but built with a huskier strength than her husband's lean power, Luke sat beside her, his long legs not having quite enough room behind the glass coffee table. "I can't tell you anything, Jenny. This is between you and Christopher."

She shook her head. "It's so confusing sometimes. I'm not sure what to do, or what to say, or how to act."

Luke shifted, facing her, his knee grazing hers. "Follow your instincts. And what's in your heart."

His green gaze was so kind, his voice so compassionate... A picture flashed in front of her with such blinding clarity she had to close her eyes. It was Luke. Not in a suit but in a red polo shirt and jeans. He was sitting on the love seat with her, handing her a present, a small box. She could see herself unwrapping it. It was a pin, a gold circle with pearls around it. And she heard Luke's voice. "I wanted to get you a birthday present as elegant as you are."

"Jenny? Jenny, what's wrong? You're as white as—"

"I remembered something! You...me...sitting here. You gave me a pin for my birthday!"

Luke jumped up. "I'll go get Christopher."

She grabbed his hand. "No. I mean, it's not very much..."

"But it's a start. Don't move."

She closed her eyes again, hoping the images would return, that she'd see more...remember more. But nothing else came and when Christopher rushed into the room with Luke, she looked up and said, "It was just a flash."

"Tell me," he demanded, sitting beside her, but not touching her.

She related what she remembered, describing the pin, what Luke was wearing, and what he'd said.

"You don't remember anyone else being here?"

"There wasn't anyone else. I mean, I could only see me and Luke. Am I right?"

"I don't know. I got tied up at the last minute and had to fly to Los Angeles."

Luke said, "I gave you my present before dinner that day...because you were upset Christopher couldn't be here. Aunt Marjorie and Uncle Wayne gave you their present later."

She remembered her joy over Luke's gift, not her disappointment at Christopher's absence that day. Yet she did feel disappointment and realized it was a present emotion, not a past one. Apparently Christopher had missed her birthday.

"You don't remember the next day?" her husband asked. "I caught the red-eye and brought you roses and perfume."

She shook her head.

The pain in Christopher's eyes hurt her and she knew the source. She remembered Luke; she didn't remember her husband. "I must have remembered because of Luke sitting beside me in this room the same way he did that evening."

"You don't have to explain. The picture is getting very clear. For whatever reason, your mind has blanked me out."

"Christopher..."

He stood and went to the hall, tossing over his shoulder, "Why don't you talk to Luke a little longer. Maybe more will come back."

Starting after his cousin, Luke said, "Christopher, don't

be an..." But his cousin's steps already sounded farther down the hall.

Luke returned to Jenny with a frown. "I don't know whether to go after him or stay with you."

"Go. I understand how frustrated he is. He needs to let it out with someone he can trust, and he trusts you. I don't know why, but he doesn't trust me. I'll be fine. I just need to sit here a few minutes."

"You're sure?"

Somewhere she found a smile to reassure him. "I'm sure."

After Luke left, Jenny closed her eyes and tried to sort all the feelings inside her. She felt attached to Christopher in a deep, elemental way that came from more than waking up and learning he was her husband. But there was a haze around that attachment, something not quite right. She thought about her first night home, when she'd been in the tub and he'd walked in. But she couldn't call her panic a memory when she wasn't sure it was. Tonight, with Luke, she'd seen him so clearly...

Why couldn't she remember Christopher that way?

Looking down at her hands folded in her lap, she realized she wasn't wearing any rings. Certainly she'd had a wedding band, perhaps an engagement ring. Had she been wearing them when her car ran off the road?

Or had she taken them off before she'd left for Binghamton?

Another question she needed to ask her husband.

The rest of the night seemed to span a century. Christopher spoke with his father and friends, acting as if the world were spinning normally. Luke had given him hell, as well he should have. After Christopher had stormed out of the Florida room, he'd realized it had been the wrong thing to do. But pride had kept him walking, kept him silent as Luke had said his two cents. It had also kept him from pulling Jenny aside and apologizing.

She'd remembered Luke and not him!

That had been a blow he'd had to absorb and accept. Just as he'd had to accept her amnesia.

He was also beginning to see a picture of his marriage he didn't like.

Before Jenny's accident, he'd never really realized how much he'd left her alone. How day after day and night after night, she'd had to find something to occupy her. He'd never thought she'd minded. She'd never complained. She'd supported his success, attending cocktail parties and dinners with him when he wasn't working late, always gracious, always acting as if there were no place else she'd rather be.

But now he wondered.

Success had always been important to him, not just to increase his income, but as a goal so he could make his mark...a place for himself in the world. He'd chosen Jenny to stand beside him. But now he didn't know if that's where she wanted to be.

And if she ever remembered everything...

He might have his answers, but no marriage.

After the men had talked of downsizing and mergers and interest rates until their cigars burnt low, they joined the women in the living room. Jenny was sitting by Marjorie with a too-bright smile on her face. Christopher could see the evening had taken its toll. The pretty pink color had left her cheeks, and he knew she was tired.

Crossing to her, he asked, "Are you ready to go?"

"Oh, Christopher, must you..." his mother began but then glanced at Jenny. "You look so lovely, my dear, I forget you're still recuperating."

Jenny rose to her feet and took Marjorie's hand. "I had a nice time. Thank you for inviting us."

Wayne came over to his son. "Marge, you stay with our guests. I'll see them out."

Marjorie reminded Jenny, "And I'll see you Wednesday for lunch. You just let me know if you want our driver to pick you up."

After a round of good-nights, Christopher and Jenny walked with his father to the foyer. As the maid brought Jenny's coat to her, before Christopher had the chance, his father took it and helped his daughter-in-law into it.

Wayne asked, "Will you be taking that trip to London now that Jenny's home?"

"I haven't decided yet," Christopher responded with a shake of his head to his father, telling him he didn't want to discuss it now.

"Were you planning a trip before my accident?" she asked.

When he'd told her about his proposed trip, she'd asked him to postpone it until summer. He had been unwilling to change his plans. But her accident had given him no choice. "Yes, I was. To open a foreign branch of Langston Financial."

"Setting up the foreign office could take six weeks or more," his father elaborated. "But if Jenny's on the mend and she certainly looks as if she is—"

"I've put the idea on hold," Christopher said.

"But you insisted you had to take advantage of the opportunities while the economic climate..."

"Dad, this really isn't the time to discuss this. Jenny's been home less than a week."

Jenny patted Wayne's arm. "With my memory loss, we have to get adjusted to each other again."

"So take her along and make it a second honeymoon!"

Christopher respected his father but at the moment, he'd like to muzzle him.

With a smile Jenny said, "Mr. Langston, if Christopher and I took a second honeymoon, I don't think I'd want him to be setting up another branch of his firm."

Wayne grinned. "You have a point there. Okay, I'll butt out. But Jenny, if you can't call me Dad, how about Wayne?"

"I'd like to call you Dad. I haven't had a father for a long time." Then she gave him a hug.

Christopher had never seen his father look so pleased. Jenny had called him Wayne before. On some level, did she realize he'd always treated her like a daughter?

On the drive home, Christopher glanced at Jenny several times. She'd closed her eyes and rested her head against the seat. They had to talk, but he wanted to wait until he could see her face.

"Do you mind if I just drive around to the back and put this in the garage? We can go in that way."

"That's fine."

Christopher pushed the garage door opener and pulled inside. Before he could come around and open her door, Jenny had hopped out. The garage seemed empty without a second car, and he knew as soon as she was able to drive, she'd need one. "We can pick out a car for you tomorrow if you'd like," he offered.

"I should be able to drive again after my next appointment with Dr. Coswell. You don't work on Saturdays?"

Christopher felt himself flush in the dim light of the garage. Usually, he did work Saturday mornings which sometimes stretched into the afternoons. "I thought we could spend the day together tomorrow. It's late to get your photographs out tonight..."

Her expression told him more clearly than words that she thought he might have forgotten.

"Let's go inside," he said, his voice gruffer than he intended.

They walked through the kitchen and dining room in silence. In the foyer, Jenny shrugged out of her coat and hung it in the closet. Christopher felt awkward, not knowing how to say what had to be said. Loosening his tie, he waited for her at the foot of the stairs.

When she came over to him, he knew he had to just get it out or she'd go to her room and close the door. "I shouldn't have left you like I did tonight. It was the wrong thing to do."

"You were upset I remembered Luke rather than you. I understand."

That aspect of Jenny's personality was the same. She always had been understanding, but he was beginning to wonder if he'd taken advantage of that, if he'd taken too much for granted. "If I had stayed with you, if we had talked about it, you might have remembered more."

"Maybe. Maybe not. I have the feeling that deliberately trying to remember won't work. Like tonight, it'll take me by surprise and just come."

"And you'll tell me when it happens? No matter what the memories are?"

"Of course, I will. Christopher, why wouldn't I?"

Because they might be too private. Because they might split their marriage in two. "Because of the way I reacted tonight. Promise me you'll tell me everything you remember."

"I promise."

Jenny's eyes were such a clear beautiful blue...with no shadows...no secrets. His palms tingled with the desire to slide down her bare arms. To unhook and unzip that dress.

The style was so simple, yet so revealing. It was much sexier than anything she'd ever worn. He swore he could see her nipples under the fabric, yet not quite. When he'd first seen her in it, he'd suspected she'd bought it for another man's pleasure.

Yet tonight she'd chosen to wear it with him. Because it was new? Because her taste was different now? Because he might respond to her in it? *Wishful thinking?*

Taking the chance he wasn't completely off course, he ran his thumb along the edge of the halter that disappeared under her arm. "Are you wearing a bra under this?"

Her eyes widened either from the question or his touch. "Yes. It's a special kind. It was hanging with the dress. But there's not much to it," she added on a whisper.

The thought of a wisp of a bra, no bra at all, brought his hands to her arms. He touched her from the edge of the halter to her wrists, his gaze holding hers, his heart pounding faster.

"Christopher, where's my wedding ring?"

Thoughts of a night of passion abruptly veered in another direction. "Your wedding band and your engagement ring are in the safe. The nurse took them off when you were admitted to the hospital. Do you want to wear them?" His heart took a hopeful leap.

"I don't think I should. Not yet. I don't *feel* married."

"We could remedy that," he said as he drew her into his arms and coaxed her lips with his.

He heard her quick intake of breath and took advantage of the moment by slipping his tongue into her mouth. The sweet, erotic taste of her so aroused him he didn't think past the immediate present and his need for the woman he'd desired for years. When her hands crept up his chest to his shoulders, he relished her touch, wanting more of it. They hadn't made love since weeks before her accident. There had been a tension between them that had kept him on his side of the bed and Jenny on hers. He'd come home after she was asleep. And if she wasn't actually asleep, she'd pretended to be.

Kissing Jenny had always been so much more than foreplay, or duty, or something married couples did. It had always been a completion, a satisfaction, a fulfillment. And now...the kiss was familiar, yet new, exciting and intoxicating, leading them where he wanted them to go.

Of their own accord, his hands wandered to the bare skin of her back. As he pressed closer into her softness, he caressed her waist, her derriere, cupping her bottom so she'd know the extent of his desire.

For a few explosive seconds, she cradled him and rubbed her breasts against his chest. But when he passed his hands up her back and his fingers worked the hooks of her dress, she pushed away.

"Marriage...marriage means more than sleeping together." Her voice trembled with the passion they'd stirred up.

He released her, realizing she was saying no, realizing much more. "It could be a start," he suggested tersely.

She looked sad and hopeful and uncertain, all at the same time. "I don't believe you can start with sex. That's not enough to build on."

Holding on to patience that was fast slipping away, he returned, "Jenny, we have more than sex. We have a life."

"A life I don't remember. I asked you for time, Christopher. I still need it. Now that I've remembered *something*, maybe I'll get it all back. I want to be fair to you. I want to be fair to us."

Examining his own motives, he suddenly knew the sense of urgency he was feeling had to do with wanting to forge a bond with her *before* she remembered. Had he always used making love to cement their relationship? Had he thought that was enough? If he successfully seduced her and she wasn't ready, he'd do more harm than good.

He tipped her chin up and searched her face. Then he kissed her lightly on the lips. "I'll get the rings from the safe, and you can put them in your jewelry chest. Maybe if you slip them on now and then, you'll remember the promises we made. Maybe you'll realize passion can be a powerful bond."

As he went to his office for the rings, *he* remembered the promise he'd made to have and to hold. Maybe he'd done a very poor job of holding.

The dream came like a shadow but shook Jenny with the force of a strong arm. It was her mother again, and a tunnel, and the figure of a man...

When she opened her eyes, she was sitting upright in her bed and shaking so hard she had to take three deep breaths in order to still her trembling.

What was the dream? What filled her with such anxiety and fear?

Should she tell Christopher? Should she go to his room?

Remembering the kiss that had punctuated their roller-coaster evening together, she doubted the wisdom of that idea. His touch, his voice, and especially his kiss, were becoming irresistible. But her upbringing or her values or some distant memory kept her cautious, hesitant and some-times downright afraid.

She wasn't afraid of Christopher, of that she was certain. But she was afraid of something that was as intangible as that shadowy man in her dream.

Slipping out of bed, she went to the dresser and opened the jewelry box. In the corner lay a diamond wedding band and a two-carat, pear-cut engagement ring. When Christopher had handed them to her earlier, she'd known they'd both hoped for some sign of recognition. She'd slid them on briefly, but they were simply a set of beautiful rings, nothing more.

With a sigh, she closed the lid on the jewelry box, knowing she wouldn't get any more sleep tonight. So...she knew exactly what she wanted to do. Develop her pictures. She'd set up the darkroom yesterday afternoon after her supplies had arrived. But before she could start developing, she'd had to get ready for the party.

She'd just pulled a pair of jeans from her closet, when she thought she heard the doorbell. It must be her imagination. But as she slipped on her robe and opened her bedroom door, she heard a pounding downstairs.

Rushing down the steps, she turned on the foyer and porch lights and gazed through the peephole in the door. It was a cowboy! At least it looked like a cowboy. The man wore a black Stetson, work shirt, jeans and boots. The slightly squared jaw looked familiar...

The picture in her wallet. This must be Christopher's cousin Jud. Without giving her action a second thought, she opened the door wide.

"Hey, Jenny. Got a spare bunk where a cowpoke can crash?"

Jud was almost as tall as Christopher, his shoulders as broad, his stomach as flat. Her husband had mentioned this cousin was two years younger than his thirty-three, but there was a seriousness in this man's eyes, a set to his mouth that made him look older.

"You must be Jud. Come on in. Christopher's sleeping..."

Jud swore and swiped his hat from his head as he stepped inside. "I forgot you wouldn't remember me."

Apparently Christopher had spoken to Jud since she'd

awakened from the coma. "I have a picture of you with Luke and Christopher. He didn't expect you yet."

"Yeah, well, for a change everything went smoothly and I was able to get away sooner than I expected. Fred helped me unload Best Chance."

"Best Chance?"

"Christopher's new horse. I left the trailer down at the stables. Better keep your distance. I drove straight through except for a few hours now and then at rest stops, so I need a shower and a change of clothes before I'm fit for a lady's company. If you just show me which room you want me to take…"

"Which do you need more? Sleep or food?" she asked with a smile. Something told her a man like Jud could pack away more than a few burgers at a time, and he probably drove the last stretch just to get where he was going.

He ran his hand through his black hair, his blue eyes twinkling. "I never turn down food. But I don't want you to drag Pauline up here on my account."

"I don't intend to. I'm capable of scrambling eggs and popping bread in the toaster!"

With a look of chagrin, he apologized. "I…uh…I'm sorry if I insulted you, but I've never seen you cook."

She laughed. "Chances are, I haven't in the past four years. But if I can figure out how to turn on the stove, there's no reason I can't now. C'mon."

Jud followed her to the kitchen. As she opened the refrigerator and found the eggs, he asked, "So you really don't remember anything after your college graduation?"

Opening one cupboard after another until she saw a bowl, she shook her head. "Last night I had a brief flash and remembered something about Luke, but nothing else."

Jud's expression was wry. "Sure. Luke. All the ladies think *he's* memorable."

"It wasn't like that. It was the compassion in his voice or something…"

Jud was beside her in a moment. "That was meant to be a joke, but your amnesia is nothing to joke about. Blame it on not enough sleep or being in the company of horses and cows for too many hours, days, and years."

There was a rough and rugged quality about Jud, yet she could tell from his reaction that he had a good heart. "Don't worry about it. I'm a lot tougher than I look."

He stepped back and studied her with eyes that seemed to see right through her. "You're different."

She sighed and looked to heaven. "*That* is becoming an old song. What do you want in your omelet? Onions, mushrooms, peppers?"

"All of the above."

Laughing, she said, "I'll see what I can find."

As the coffee perked and the omelet sizzled, Jenny drew Jud out, learning about the Star Four and the horses he trained. He was less talkative than Christopher and Luke, in many ways less social. But he was used to a different type of life where a man's next meal could depend on the weather, the price of cattle, or the hardiness of a new foal. More primitive. That was the word she wanted. But she liked Jud.

He was forking in his second helping of omelet, she was sipping coffee, when Christopher appeared in the doorway to the kitchen. Surprise crossed his face first but then it was followed by a wariness that swept over her satin robe, the meal on the table, and Jud's black Stetson sitting on the counter. "I smelled coffee but never expected to find breakfast for two. Isn't this cozy?"

"I didn't want to wake you. You've gotten to bed late the past few nights…" She trailed off, feeling as if she'd done something wrong again but not sure what.

"I don't need much sleep, Jenny."

The implication was she didn't remember *that,* either. Standing, she motioned to the plates on the table. "There's a wedge of omelet left if you want it. I'll be in the darkroom if you need me for anything." As she slipped by her husband she said in a mock whisper, "You might want to rethink how much sleep you *do* need. A little more and you might not be so grouchy when you get up."

Then she left the kitchen before either man could react. Because she was sure they both would.

Chapter Five

"What in blue blazes was *that* all about?" Jud asked with a hard stare.

"I don't know what you mean," Christopher muttered, still trying to put the early morning into perspective. He'd awakened, planning to kiss Jenny good morning, then go for a jog. But instead, when he'd gone to her room, he'd found it empty again. He'd hurried downstairs, fearing once more that her memory had returned and she'd left to spend her life with someone else. Damn, but he felt rattled, and seeing her in her nightgown with Jud, talking and laughing...

"The hell you don't know what I mean!" Jud growled. "Either you intended to insult me or your wife, but we both got a shovelful. I've got to hand it to her. She put you in your place with a lot more sugar than I was going to."

"She's different than she used to be."

"*She's* got amnesia. What's your excuse?"

Christopher had always admired Jud's no-nonsense, get-to-the-point attitude. But this morning it irritated him. "You don't know the whole story."

Jud leaned back in his chair and crossed his arms over his chest. "So fill me in. I'm not going anywhere but to bed. I've kept my eyes open this long, another hour isn't going to make a difference."

Christopher realized that he, Luke and Jud had never kept secrets from each other. Even when Jud had taken off for the northwest last year and hadn't told his father where he'd ended up, Christopher and Luke had known where to reach him. And it was a good thing, too. Thatcher Whitmore's brush with death had brought Jud back home to a birthright he'd finally come to accept.

They'd all been pals. They'd worked and raised hell together summer after summer. But the words that would tell Jud his most private demon still stuck in Christopher's throat. He'd called Jud about Jenny's accident, later told him she had amnesia but hadn't revealed the suspicion plaguing him. Finally after he'd poured a mug of coffee, he got it out. "Before Jenny's accident, I think she was having an affair."

Jud's response was immediate. "No way!"

Christopher sat across from his cousin and set his mug on the table. "There were hang-up calls. She was edgy...faraway. When I brought up having a baby, she closed down the discussion before it could even get going."

"Did you let it drop?"

"You know Jenny. She said we had plenty of time, she became even more quiet..."

"She got more quiet as the years passed."

"Meaning?"

Jud shrugged. "I'm not sure."

"Tell me what you saw, Jud. I was working long hours. I'm just realizing how little I paid attention."

"I think she gave up."

"Gave up what?" he asked, not understanding.

"Trying to get your attention," Jud answered. "All Jenny ever wanted to do was make you happy. *That* was obvious. You were seven years older, successful, and needed a socially acceptable woman to be the perfect partner. And she was. She came from a good background, was educated, beautiful, gracious and worked hard at being exactly what you wanted her to be."

Jud's assessment shocked Christopher. His pride made him defensive. "I gave Jenny anything she could possibly want. She never complained. She never said she wasn't happy."

"I think she *was* happy being the wife she thought you wanted. I'm just telling you what I saw. But even if she'd decided she *wasn't* happy, I can't see her having an affair. Not Jenny. She's not that type of woman."

Jud's attitude surprised Christopher. His cousin's outlook on women was usually cynical, not optimistic. Christopher pushed away the coffee mug, deciding he didn't need another bitter taste in his mouth. "What else could it be?"

"She doesn't remember anything?"

He grimaced and thought about last night. "Just Luke."

"Yeah, she told me. And you resent it."

Sometimes Jud saw entirely too much. But then *he* could be objective right now. He didn't have a wife to lose. "What else did she tell you? I never know what's going to come out of her mouth these days."

"Not much. But I got to tell you, pal. I like her this way. She's like the old Jenny. But better." Jud sipped his coffee and leaned his chair back on two legs. "So what are you going to do about all of it? If she doesn't remember anything she might have done…"

If only it were that simple. If only he could forget, too.

"There was another hang-up call a few days ago. If she was seeing somebody, he'll contact her. I'd bet my life on it."

"Your life or your marriage?" Jud asked with a raised brow.

Christopher raked his hand through his hair. "I want her, Jud. I just don't know if I can live with the doubts. And if she remembers…"

"All your problems could be solved. You'll find out you were wrong."

He hoped to God Jud was right. But he had the feeling if Jenny remembered, all his problems might just begin.

After Jud crashed in a guest bedroom, Christopher showered, called Luke, dressed in a T-shirt and jeans, then went to find his wife. As he loped down the stairs to her office, she emerged from her darkroom.

She saw him and stopped. "I wanted to make sure Jud had everything he needed."

"He's fine. He set the alarm for eleven. He said if he sleeps too long now, he won't be able to sleep tonight."

"How long is he staying?"

"Monday morning. He's afraid if he's away too long, Uncle Thatcher will make a decision without him. Those two could argue from dusk till dawn if given half a reason."

"But they live together, don't they?" she asked.

"You could say that. Mostly they try to stay out of each other's way. Uh, I thought since Jud's sleeping we could look at cars."

"Wouldn't you rather go look at or ride your new horse?"

Of course he would. But he'd made a promise and he was going to keep it. "I told you we'd find you a car."

"That was before you knew Jud would be here. Does Luke know Jud arrived?"

"I called him. If he gets here before we get back, he can keep Jud company."

"Christopher, I don't need to look at cars today. Go on down to the stable until Jud wakes up or Luke gets here." When he hesitated, she said, "Really. I don't mind. I'm going out on Monday. I'll look at cars then."

"By yourself?"

"You don't think a woman can cut as good a deal as a man?" There was challenge in her tone, but a hint of amusement, too.

"I'm not sticking my foot in that one," he said with a smile. Then he thought about what she'd said. "Where are you going Monday?"

"I need mats for the pictures I'm developing. I saw Seneft's Gallery now has a mount and frame shop."

Suddenly he remembered something else he'd said they'd do. "Let's go look at your photographs. It won't be hot in the attic this time of day."

"Won't we wake Jud?"

"He could sleep through a world war. Besides, we'll be on the other side of the house."

"What about Best Chance?"

"Best Chance can wait until we sort through your photographs." He impulsively snagged her hand. "C'mon."

She looked at her hand in his and gave him a smile that was so genuinely pleased it made him ache. Then she squeezed his fingers. "All right. Let's go see if we can find something to decorate my walls."

With her hand in Christopher's, Jenny walked beside him through the house until they came to the attic door. She knew he hoped this trip to the third floor would produce more than pictures for her walls. She wanted to remember her life with him, all the emotions she must have felt.

He paused at the door and drew her close. There was turmoil in his brown eyes. Something he wanted to say. But instead of speaking, he bent his head and kissed her. It was a much different kiss from last night's, filled with sweetness and desire and longing. When he raised his head, he released her hand and opened the door.

Five pine steps led to a landing. Seven more steps turned, reaching to the attic floor. Sunlight streamed in the front set of gable windows as Christopher motioned to the back where she spotted several cardboard boxes.

A small Victorian love seat from her mother's house stood under the eaves partially covered by a sheet. Christopher whisked off the covering and motioned for Jenny to sit.

She took little notice of the other odds and ends of furniture, the other cartons. All of her attention focused on her husband as he took framed and matted photographs from a box and laid them on the floor in front of her.

Studying the photographs, she immediately noticed a few she'd taken in college. She tried to remember a time and place for each of the others. While she concentrated so hard on one of three children cavorting on a jungle gym, her eyes started to blur.

Christopher said gently, "Relax, Jenny. Just see if any one of them triggers something."

When he continued to place photographs before her that weren't framed, she wondered what he was thinking...if any of the pictures meant something to him. She seemed to favor children and animals and bucolic settings. But then Christopher produced one of a stormy sky, a set of photographs in a city—of street vendors, and the homeless, and a theater front that had seen better days.

"New York City?" she asked.

Christopher nodded.

With no feelings stirring, no recognition, she was disappointed. "What about photographs of us...on our honeymoon, vacations..."

"Our personal albums are downstairs."

"Let's look at those. Just leave these and I'll pick out the ones I want to use later."

"I could carry them down to your office."

"Most of the ones I like aren't framed."

He studied her, surrounded by the photographs, another link to the years she couldn't remember. "Our photo albums are in the top of my closet in the bedroom. Would you like me to get them?"

She nodded.

As Christopher went downstairs, she thought about what could happen if they looked at the photos together in the bedroom, the bed a few feet away. All too easily she could see Christopher kissing her, almost feel his hands on her skin...

Was it a memory or a wish?

He returned a few minutes later with three albums. One was large and leather-bound. Taking that one from him, she opened it and studied pictures of their wedding. Page after page she touched and searched for a hint of something. Anything. But her smiles and Christopher's seemed to belong to another couple. When she turned to a large photograph of her standing with her mother, her heart beat faster and her temples pounded.

"What is it, Jenny?"

"I...uh, I don't know. Maybe it's just that I miss her so much..." She suddenly glimpsed a scene in this attic at another time. A shoe box. She was sitting on the floor, boxes and cards and papers all around her. Up here. Closing her eyes, she saw herself slip a letter from an envelope. Then nothing. Nothing.

Christopher turned her face toward him, his fingers gentle on her chin. "Jenny?"

Her heart still pounded. Anxiety filled her, like the anxiety she'd felt her first day home with Christopher—when he'd come into the bathroom, and when she'd thought he was going to kiss her. She pulled away from him again...confused. And immediately saw the worry on his face.

"I remember being up here. Going through boxes of letters, cards..."

"We took care of all your mother's important papers immediately. Being a lawyer, she was well organized and kept anything vital in her desk. But she'd kept boxes of personal correspondence over the years as well—cards and letters from you and your father, from friends. We had so much to take care of after her death, it was difficult for you to go through those, too. So we brought the boxes up here. Last year, you started reading them and sorting. You ended up with that one box over there."

She felt shaken without knowing why. Taking a full, bolstering breath, she closed the album. "Do you mind if we do this later? I could use some fresh air. Let's go look at Best Chance."

He didn't touch her but he looked as if he wanted to. "Talk to me, Jenny. Don't close me out."

Tears came to her eyes. "I'm *not* closing you out. It's like I remember something, yet I don't. It's so hard to understand."

He put his arm around her then, squeezing her close, not giving her the chance to pull away. "Do you want to call Dr. Coswell?"

This time she didn't want to pull away. Christopher was

strength and caring and stability, and no matter what she felt before, her feelings for him now were growing deeper each day. "No, I don't have to call her. I think this is what she meant by memory fragments. I just have to let them come and hope that they all join together."

Christopher rested his chin on top of her head and was silent. She knew they were both hoping she'd remember soon.

Music blared from the speakers on the stage where a four-piece band played popular hits on Saturday evening. Jud sat across from Jenny and Christopher, a scowl on his face. "I don't know why I let you pull me out to a place like this every time I come to town."

"You had to eat," Christopher pointed out with a grin.

"Seems to me there was plenty of food back at the house. Pauline keeps your refrigerator stocked," he grumbled.

"Luke and I decided years ago that when we get the opportunity to put you in a civilized environment away from cows and horses, we should do it. Look around, Cowboy, and broaden your horizon."

Jud's gaze narrowed as he picked up his last cheese fry and poked it into his mouth. "You and Luke brought me here for more than the food and you know it. If I didn't like you as much as I do, I'd dance with your wife for the evening and let *you* fend off the polished career-types Luke always wants to introduce me to. Any of the women in here wouldn't be caught dead mucking out a stall or sleeping on a bedroll under the stars."

Jenny's arm comfortably brushed Christopher's as she turned in her chair to quickly canvas the room. "I don't know, Jud. That brunette Luke's talking to looks as if she could heave a pitchfork with the best of them."

Jud shook his finger at her. "Don't tell me you're in cahoots with the two of *them*. I was counting on you to be on my side."

"I *am* on your side. But this afternoon Luke told me you work too hard and need to have some fun."

"Seems to me that applies to someone else I know," he retorted with a pointed look at Christopher.

But Christopher wasn't taking the bait. He was wrestling with his own devils in that arena. That's why he'd insisted Jenny come with them tonight. He wanted her to have some fun. For both of them to have fun together.

Just then, Luke came back to the table with a lithe, slim blonde, who'd curved her hand over his arm. The brunette Jenny had noticed was also with him. "Everyone, this is Sharon." He slid his arm around the blonde's waist. "She's an old friend." Then he nodded to Jud. "And, Cous, this is Tamara. She assures me she knows how to do the Texas two-step, and if we can convince the band to play something appropriate, you've got a partner."

Christopher watched Jud assess the brunette and give a small shrug. "I'm game for the two-step and anything slow."

As if on cue, the band started a ballad that could definitely fit Jud's definition of slow.

Luke's arched brows and I-dare-you expression made Jud get to his feet and ask Tamara, "Would you like to dance?"

Luke bent to Christopher and Jenny. "We'll see you two later."

Christopher laughed. "Luke always could get Jud to do things I couldn't."

Jenny leaned close to him so he could hear her above the music. "Thanks for including me tonight. I enjoyed hearing about your summers on the Star Four."

Her hair practically brushed his cheek, her perfume wound around his head, and his laughter slipped away. "I was hoping you wouldn't be bored."

She smiled. "Not likely."

That smile... He needed her in his arms. "Would you like to dance?"

When she nodded, he quickly pushed back his chair then guided her to the dance floor. Taking her in his arms, he drew her close. She was sunshine and smiles and woman—all he'd ever wanted in a wife. Maybe he'd never realized that before. He'd taken so much for granted. Not only her commitment to their marriage, but her presence at the end of each day, her ability to make him feel he was the priority in her life. At least she had until the last six months.

Had she told him the truth up in the attic today? Or had she remembered more than she was letting on?

She'd worn a silky blouse tonight in a rose color that perfectly matched her slacks. He could feel the press of her breasts against his shirt and his body stirred.

Putting an inch or two between them, he cleared his throat and said, "You always got along with Luke, but this visit, you and Jud seem to have a lot to talk about." Earlier in the afternoon, after he'd put Best Chance through his paces, he and Luke had gone riding. When they'd returned, Jud and Jenny had been involved in a lively discussion about how Jud trained young horses.

Jenny's hand slid farther back on Christopher's shoulder, alerting every nerve in his body. He'd worn the tan, collarless shirt as a change from his usual suit and tie. But her fingers were close to his neck, and the idea of her touching him there made the heat on the dance floor go up a few notches.

Tilting her head up, she met his gaze. "I like Luke, but...he looks at me the way you do sometimes. Like he knows a secret about me. Jud…he just seems to take me as I am.''

So forthright…so open about her thoughts. Had loneliness made her keep them more and more to herself? Had she believed he didn't want to hear what she'd been thinking?

Jud believed in Jenny's loyalty. Christopher wished belief was as easy as a decision. "I don't want any secrets between us, Jenny."

"But there will be until I remember, won't there?"

It wasn't an easy question and he didn't have an easy answer. Without a reply, he drew her closer again, needing to feel connected, hoping to find the bond they once shared. Instead, he found heated desire. He couldn't be this close and not want to take her to bed.

Aroused, there was no way he could hide it. "I want you," he murmured into her ear. He felt the tremor that ran through her and hoped she was thinking the same erotic thoughts he was. As he kissed her cheek, her arms wrapped around his neck. He nibbled the corner of her lips, and her eyes closed as they swayed to the music.

"Maybe we should go back to the table," she said with as much breathlessness as he felt.

"You don't like dancing with me like this?" He couldn't help testing the honesty between them further.

"I like it," she murmured close to his jaw. "But I don't want you to think this is going to lead us…"

When her voice caught, he finished for her. "You don't want me to think this will lead us to bed." He felt her push away slightly, and he wondered if honesty could become a wall between them, too.

Then with totally unexpected tenderness toward him, she stroked his jaw. "I'm hoping I soon remember everything. I don't want any secrets between us, either."

And if she did remember everything?

He kissed her then, in the middle of the dance floor, telling himself that having her in his arms this close, as arousing and frustrating as it was to know he couldn't take his desire any further, was better than feeling her slip away.

When Luke and his partner brushed by them, Christopher hardly noticed. He was too busy savoring the moment and chastising himself for not having done so in the past.

Early Monday morning, Christopher and Luke walked Jud to his truck and trailer. Luke had joined them for breakfast, and Jenny had already hugged Jud and said goodbye.

Jud's Stetson was low on his forehead as he opened the truck door.

Luke lodged one foot on the runner. "It's a shame you have to leave so soon. We could play another round of tennis. Or better yet, I could introduce you to another of Sharon's friends."

Smiling to himself, Christopher shook his head. His mother and father had asked them all over for tennis and dinner yesterday. But Jud was much more comfortable riding a fence line. And as far as another introduction to a woman Luke considered suitable for his cousin... Jud had danced with Tamara a few times, then left the club with Christopher and Jenny, preferring their company. So he'd said.

Jud frowned as he answered Luke. "If I don't get back, Dad might overdo it. Mack's supposed to keep him in line, but he can only do so much. And as far as you matching me up again..." He gave his cousin a wry twist of his mouth. "You don't know my type."

"What is your type?" Christopher asked, really wanting to know.

There was a good minute of silence.

"Damned if I know." Jud swiped off his hat and spun it on his hand. "Or maybe I do. I did something stupid."

"What kind of something?" Luke asked before Christopher could.

Jud's hand stilled and his blue eyes met Christopher's. "Remember that night you called me to tell me Dad had a heart attack?"

"On that ranch in Montana?" That night was hard for Christopher to forget. He'd received a frantic call from Thatcher's housekeeper, who'd been looking for Jud. He'd anxiously made the call to Montana, reminding himself his cousin wasn't using his given name but rather his initials in order to give himself a new identity.

"Yeah. Well, the guy who answered...when he came to get me he almost found me...us..." Jud swore. "I slept with a twenty-one-year-old virgin. Without protection."

The three of them had made a pact years ago that they'd be careful—always—for their sake and the woman's. If Jud hadn't been careful, Christopher bet there was a good reason...even if his cousin didn't know it yet. "Is that the end of it?"

"I left that night. She doesn't even know my last name. You know, I was going by J.T.... And I left without talking to her again."

Luke took his foot from the truck runner. "You never told her where you lived?"

"Every year, *you* go somewhere and pretend you're a general contractor. I wanted to be someone other than Judson Thatcher Whitmore, heir to the Star Four."

"What are you going to do?" Christopher was concerned about Jud. Since his father's heart attack, he'd taken on burdens and responsibilities he'd accepted but didn't really want.

"I think about calling her...writing to her, but she's ten

years younger.'' He shook his head. ''It might be better to let well enough alone.'' With a shrug, he said, ''It's not your problem. I've got to shove off.'' Slapping his hat back on his head, he clapped Luke on the back, then Christopher. ''Come visit, you two. You can distract my dad so he stays out of my hair.''

With the flash of a grin that Christopher saw all too rarely from Jud, his cousin climbed into his truck and slammed the door.

Luke and Christopher watched him pull away.

''Whoever she was, she got to him,'' Luke said.

Christopher kept silent, but he absolutely agreed.

Late on Monday morning, Jenny paid the cab driver and got out in front of Seneft's Gallery, thinking about the weekend. Saturday night had been...tempting. Christopher had been irresistible and sexy, and her heart stirred with feelings that couldn't be possible in merely a week. Her heart and soul knew him even if *she* didn't remember knowing him. They had had such a nice weekend.

Yesterday Christopher's parents had invited them all to dinner, before which she and Marjorie had watched Jud, Luke, Christopher and his father play tennis. The afternoon had been filled with sunshine and laughter. Jud looked nothing like a cowboy in tennis shorts and a shirt borrowed from Christopher, with a racket in hand borrowed from Luke. In fact, Jenny sensed Jud hid behind the strong, silent, rough facade to protect himself. She hadn't discovered why.

Hopefully, he'd visit again. Or maybe they'd visit him... She suddenly realized she wanted a future with Christopher, if only he'd tell her what was bothering him. Tell her what stood between them. Because she could feel something did.

Seneft's Gallery had been a favorite hangout of Jenny's

during her vacations home from college. She'd loved spending time just contemplating the composition of the paintings, photographs and sculptures on display. But when she walked inside now, she realized the gallery she'd known had changed. There were more walls, more space between the frames, and pottery rather than sculptures. A doorway led into another room which used to be the store next door. In that area samples of frames hung on the wall in all shapes, sizes, textures and colors. Several worktables with rolls of backing paper and a staple gun manifested a do-it-yourself invitation.

She didn't recognize the man behind the counter. He was good-looking, in his mid-thirties, with a brown moustache that moved when he smiled at her. "Can I help you?"

After she set her purse on the counter, she lifted the envelope in her hand and removed the photographs. "I'd like to mat these and frame them. I understand you do that here now. When I used to come into Seneft's, it was just a gallery."

He extended his hand to her. "Dave Hedgewick. I bought out George over a year ago. The frame shop is a sign of the times. The gallery has been losing money for years. With the frame shop, I can keep it open."

Shaking his hand, she smiled, then laid the photographs in front of him. "I want to choose mats in colors of the sunset and use complementary frames. I'm thinking about two groupings."

As he studied the photographs, he reached for the stack of mat samples. Then he looked at her speculatively. "Are you an amateur or professional?"

"I've never sold any." At least she didn't think she had. "But I'd like to open my own studio."

"Do you have more?"

She laughed. "Boxes and two rolls I developed yester-day."

"Did you see the sign in the gallery?"

She'd hurried through, intending to look more carefully after she'd taken care of her pictures. "A sign?"

"I'm having an open house for new artists the weekend of May eighteenth. There's a reception on that Saturday night and the gallery will be open Sunday for browsers. Would you like to be included? As it is, I'm displaying two watercolor artists, and a potter. Your photographs would add another dimension."

"You want to display my work?"

He smiled again. "If we can get it framed and matted in time. Can you come back tomorrow with your others?"

"Sure, I can. This is wonderful!"

"It'll be even more wonderful if they sell. And I think they will. You've got talent..." He waited for her to supply her name.

"Jenny...Jenny Langston," she said.

"Christopher Langston's wife. I remember reading about your accident. Your picture ran in the paper with the news item. It sounded serious. I'm glad to see you've recovered."

"I have. Almost." She couldn't see any reason to go into her amnesia with him.

"Well, good. Let me show you around the gallery and we can discuss my commission and your profit."

As Dave Hedgewick came around from behind the desk, Jenny followed him into the gallery. She couldn't wait to tell Christopher! He'd be so proud.

In the attic, Jenny sat cross-legged on the floor, trying to decide which photographs to take to the gallery the next day. She was also thinking about the car she'd seen that would best suit her purposes when she heard Christopher's footsteps on the stairs. Looking up, she smiled as he rounded the landing and climbed toward her.

He was home before dinner. With his tie tugged down, his white shirtsleeves rolled up, he looked more relaxed than he had last week. Maybe the weekend had done that.

Coming over to her, he towered above her. "How was your day?"

She wanted to reach up, stroke his face and kiss him. Not knowing whether the inclination was from the past or in the present, and not feeling free enough to follow the impulse, she answered instead. "It was wonderful."

When he crouched down beside her, he picked up a photograph of two swans on a lake. The profile of their elegant necks formed a heart. "You found a car?"

His legs were so long, his thighs, strong and hard. She remembered his body against hers as they'd danced...

"I found one I really like. I didn't drive it yet. The salesman took me out in it. But it's everything I need. Only...it wasn't at the dealership you sent me to. This isn't a luxury car. It's a four-wheel-drive all-purpose vehicle."

He dropped the photograph. "What?"

"Oh, Christopher, it's great. The back seat folds down and I can fit my photographic equipment in easily. It will go anywhere. If I want to drive down a muddy road to get a picture, I can. It's exactly what I need."

Standing again, he dominated the attic space. "You're alive today because you were driving a solid, well-built car. I don't want you to risk safety for a popular fad."

"I didn't realize whatever car I chose would have to meet your approval. Of course I'm not going to risk my safety. I might not remember my accident, but it changed my life. I brought home information, including consumer magazines' ratings. Tell me something, Christopher. Did you always treat me like a child? And did I put up with it?''

Lines furrowed his brow and anger simmered in his eyes. "Just because I'm concerned about your safety—"

Feeling at a disadvantage, she rose to her feet. "No. You want to make decisions for me. Did I let you because you earn money and I don't?"

"This has nothing to do with money!" he exploded. "We *never* argued about money."

Toe to toe with him, she didn't back down. "I remember you said we never argued. Didn't I feel I had a right to express my opinion? Did I always do what you wanted?"

He swore and turned. "You make me sound like a controlling SOB—"

She grabbed his arm before he could walk way. "Were you?"

"No!" He clasped her shoulders. "No, I wasn't. And you weren't like this. You never questioned my motives. You trusted my judgment."

"Did you trust mine?"

"Jenny…"

"Did you? Did I ever make important decisions?" She could see him struggling with her questions, to answer them for himself as well as her.

"You made all sorts of decisions for the charities you work with and—"

"I mean in our personal lives and our marriage."

He dropped his hands and stepped away. "You didn't want to make decisions about cars and decorating. You sat back, Jenny."

"What? I married you and lost my personality?"

"Why can't you let this go?"

"Because I need to understand why I became someone

else. Why I let you run my life. Why I didn't go after my dreams.''

''Maybe your dreams changed,'' he said in a low voice filled with frustration.

So drawn toward him, yet battling to find her identity, she asked, ''Did I make you my world until nothing else mattered?''

When he studied her, she saw the realization in his eyes and heard it in his words. ''Maybe you did.''

She understood how, if she'd loved him with all her heart, his wishes and desires could have become everything. But what about hers? Had he loved her the same way? ''I imagine, it just happened. There's no one to blame,'' she said to reassure him, to reassure herself.

''No, I guess there's no one to blame for that.'' His expression had changed, becoming more shuttered.

''Whatever happened in the past, Christopher, I need to hold on to some independence now.''

''By choosing your own car.''

''That's one way. But there's more.''

''I'm afraid to ask,'' he said with a wry twist of his mouth, turmoil in his deep brown eyes.

Her accident hadn't just changed *her* life; it had changed his. Every new day was an adjustment for them both. ''I told you I had a wonderful day. I didn't just find a car.''

The afternoon heat in the attic, even though she'd opened a window and a gentle breeze billowed through, seemed to add to the tension. The silence at the top of the house magnified the vibrations between them, urging her to rediscover what they once had or to find something even better.

''When I went to the gallery, Dave liked my photographs. He wants to include my work in an open house he's having in less than three weeks. I might be able to sell them and start building a reputation.''

"Dave?" Christopher asked.

She and the gallery owner had easily related on a first-name basis. "Yes. David Hedgewick. He told me he bought the gallery from George Seneft over a year ago."

"Did you remember him?"

Not understanding the sternness in her husband's tone, she repeated, "Remember him? No. After I told him my name, he recognized me. He said my picture had been in the paper."

"Why does he want your photographs in the show?"

Christopher seemed wary...and suspicious. Her temper started to rise. "Because *he* thinks I have talent. Is that so impossible?"

"Are you sure he doesn't want your photographs because you have a name that could bring in wealthy clientele? Or because..."

This time *she* turned away and headed for the stairs. At the top one she stopped. "You know, sometimes I want to dive into your arms, and others I'd like to hit you over the head. You can be so...so...macho. I'm going to the darkroom. If you decide you can be as excited about this as I am, we can talk about it. Otherwise, you can keep your opinions to yourself."

She thought she heard him swear. She thought she heard him call her name.

But she needed the peace of her darkroom, and she hoped she could soon remember why she'd ever given it up.

Chapter Six

Jenny used to be sugar. Now she was sugar mixed with spice, frustrating him to hell and back, but Christopher had to admit he liked the combination. The problem was that if he didn't learn how to deal with her, she could leave his life—this time maybe for good.

Staring at her photographs spread on the attic floor, he realized how distinctive they all were—simple yet complex at the same time. Side lighting, or background framing or an off-center capture of her subject emphasized the talent in her composition. She didn't just snap a picture. She analyzed and shot for the best effect.

Drawn to her work in a way he never had been before, he sat where she had sat and studied each and every one of the photographs...trying to find her. Had he ever really known the woman he'd married?

Sweat beaded his brow and shadows grew longer as his stomach grumbled. He should go get Jenny and hope that he could entice her to dive into his arms instead of hitting him over the head. He practically smiled until he remembered why she'd gotten so annoyed with him. She'd had every reason...

Except...

Had she really only met David Hedgewick today? She'd gone there for an, albeit, seemingly innocent purpose. But what if she'd felt drawn there because she'd known him before?

What if Hedgewick was the man who'd called and hung up?

The idea wasn't farfetched. Jenny and this man would obviously have common interests. Although she might be unaware of a past association, the gallery owner could manipulate her into spending time with him. This open house was the perfect excuse.

Christopher suspected people had patterns, even people who had amnesia. Before his mind wandered too far afield, he should get more information and find out what he was dealing with.

A half hour and a few phone calls later, he couldn't dismiss his suspicions. Hedgewick had bought the gallery over a year ago. Instead of being elderly and married as Christopher had hoped, he'd discovered the man was thirty-six, well-educated and divorced. On top of that, the gallery owner had a brother in Elmira which wasn't that far from Binghamton.

Was he reaching? Was he being paranoid? Could it all be coincidence?

He knew he couldn't keep Jenny from being part of this artists' show. And he didn't want to if it was what she really wanted. But he *could* keep her distracted. He could convince her that their marriage could be hotter and more exciting than any affair.

Deciding no time was better than the present, he headed for her darkroom.

When he saw the light above the door was on and heard music playing inside, he knocked firmly. He felt like an intruder down here. He'd never spent much time in the sitting area or her office.

"Just a second," Jenny called. When she opened the door a few moments later, the music still blared. Quickly moving away, she turned the knob on the speaker on the wall. It was wired to the stereo unit in her office.

Photographs, attached with clothespins, hung from a line. "Can I take a look?" he asked.

She motioned to them, her attitude more cautious than welcoming. He couldn't blame her.

"They're good, Jenny."

"Some of them are. Some could be better."

"You *do* have talent. If I insulted you, I didn't mean to."

"If?" she repeated.

A fan whirled softly, the smells of the darkroom mingled with a delicate perfume, the one he'd noticed earlier when he'd climbed the steps to the attic. "I've never been very good at apologies," he admitted.

"If we never argued, I guess neither of us needed to apologize."

He couldn't tell if she was being sarcastic or sincere. Jeez, this woman threw him off balance. Crooking his finger at her, he requested, "Come here."

After a brief hesitation, she stepped close to him.

"I want you to be happy. I want you to be safe."

"And you don't want me to upset your world."

Anger rose up for an instant until he realized she was right. Her note had turned his world upside down, and it hadn't righted itself yet. Just when he felt he was getting a grasp on their life, she made it spin again. "What I want doesn't seem to matter. Between you and fate..."

"What you want matters to me," she said softly. "But what *I* want matters, too. Your respect is as important as anything else that happens between us."

"I've always respected you, Jenny."

"You know, don't you, that *you* have the advantage? I have to trust what you say to find out about myself...to learn about us. That's scary."

He had to touch her then. They were standing too close; he wanted her too much. Taking her face between his hands, he bent his head and found her lips with a hunger that should have scared him. But it didn't. It just gnawed deeper, urging him to angle her mouth so he could taste more, inflame her to the same fever pitch that pushed him, convince her that they were better together than they ever could be apart.

Music still played softly. Jenny kissed Christopher as if he were her husband instead of a man she thought she didn't know. His fingers on her face, rippling through her hair, gave her such a sense of belonging that tears came to her eyes. How could she not respond to his passion?

He was leading her deeper and deeper and deeper into it...

The kiss changed from fiery desire to pure seduction. His tongue stroked hers, teased her into playing, then withdrew. The next moment, he was laving her lower lip, stroking her hair, unbuttoning her blouse.

Suddenly she realized it was a seduction, maybe deliberate, and she couldn't let it happen. Her heart beating faster than she ever thought was possible, she leaned back and covered his hand with hers.

As he raised his head, he said, "Jenny, just let it happen."

She saw the need in his eyes and almost gave in. But

she knew if she did, there would be no turning back. She didn't trust him that much yet. Or herself.

"Is this why you came down here? So 'it' would happen?"

Instead of getting angry as she expected he might, he drew in a deep breath, then admitted, "Yes, I guess it is. I want you, Jenny. And you want me. Why shouldn't we take what we want?"

"Because it doesn't *feel* right yet, Christopher. I still have so many questions...so many pieces I can't fit into a complete picture. All I have right now where we're concerned are feelings and vague sensations. Before you knocked, I was listening to a CD that I found in the stereo in my office. It's a Broadway show. The music ties me up in knots...makes me cry. Why? Because it's so beautiful? Or because it means something special to me? Or us?" She turned up the volume on the speaker.

After a pause, he said, "You saw that play in New York in the fall."

She tried to read his expression but couldn't. "Can we go again? Maybe if I actually sit there, see it, experience it, something will come back."

The music played in the quiet. Finally Christopher agreed. "All right. When would you like to go?"

"I know it might be hard for you to get away..."

"Do you want to go as soon as I can get tickets?"

"I'd like that."

Stepping close again, he caressed her cheek. "I'll take care of it. When we're in New York, we can make some new memories instead of just trying to retrieve old ones." He dropped his hand and went to the door. "Pauline will have dinner ready soon."

"I'll be there in a few minutes. I want to clean up."

He nodded.

"You *do* think New York is a good idea, don't you?" she asked.

"I think if it's something you need to do, you should do it. I'll see you upstairs."

All she could really trust were her feelings. And right now she felt as if Christopher was keeping something from her again. Would she find out what it was in New York?

In his office the next morning, Christopher held the receiver while he waited for his mother's housekeeper to call her in from the garden. He didn't know how she'd react to his request, but he'd decided last night the best course of action to take.

Last night.

He and Jenny had eaten dinner and talked about nothing important—details of their lives. They'd discussed the horses, his work and how he invested his clients' money, Jud's visit. Then they'd taken a walk and, of all things, played Scrabble! It had been a good evening, an enjoyable evening, and when he'd kissed her good night, he thought of New York and the risk he was about to take.

It was necessary.

"Good morning, Christopher. Is something wrong?" his mother asked.

He never called his parents during the day. He usually didn't have the time. "Nothing's wrong. I have a favor to ask."

"Anything. You know that."

Remembering that his request to live at home rather than boarding school had been denied repeatedly, that when he'd asked his parents to visit the Star Four during his summers there his father had been too busy, he didn't feel confident about his mother's willingness to help him now. "You and

Jenny are having lunch tomorrow. She'll probably mention a trip to New York she and I are going to take."

"That's wonderful! It will do her a world of good. She loved the play she and I saw in the fall. It was a shame you had to cancel at the last minute and I went with her instead."

"That's my favor. Don't tell her you went with her."

"Why ever not?"

"It's complicated, Mother. But her doctor feels it's better if she remembers on her own. After we go to the play and see if it brings back any memories, I'll tell her that I didn't accompany her. But I think she needs to go to New York with a clean slate."

"Is that your only reason?"

"I don't know what you mean."

"Christopher, you know I love your father dearly, but he puts business before our personal life. You have always done the same. I wonder if Jenny's accident has shown you she's more important than any business meeting ever could be. But you can't start fresh by keeping something from her."

Christopher rested his elbow on the desk, glancing at his schedule for the day. He'd always lived by that schedule, in part because he always *had* seen his father live that way. At a young age, his dad had pointed out the benefits of working hard, mentally and physically, setting goals, and the success both would bring. Wayne Langston had never discussed with him the other side of it—how personal relationships got shuffled behind appointments and the toll that could take on a marriage.

"My situation with Jenny isn't simple. And I'm only keeping this from her until after the play. Then I'll tell her. If she doesn't remember."

"I hope you know what you're doing. I decided long

ago to accept my life with your father and not try to change him. But Jenny's a woman of a different generation. Much more vocal now than before her accident. Don't underestimate her.''

He'd never talked to his mother about his marriage. Early in his life, his parents had taught him independence and the necessity of making his own way. From the day they'd sent him to boarding school, he'd understood that he wasn't supposed to need them or their advice. But now his relationship with Jenny was at stake. "Before the accident, did Jenny ever say anything to you? Did she tell you she was unhappy?''

His mother didn't hesitate. "I think she was lonely. Believe me, I know the signs. And the past few months, I think something was bothering her. But I didn't want to pry and she never confided in me.''

"Fate has given me the opportunity to make some changes. But if she remembers...''

"She'll remember everything, Christopher. Including whatever you do, however you act from now on.''

"That's what I'm hoping.''

"Good luck, Son. I'll be praying for you.''

His mother's words brought a lump to his throat, and he wondered just how well he knew *either* of the women in his life.

Christopher tipped the bellboy, then closed the door. "Are you sure this is all right?''

Jenny couldn't believe she'd made the request to come to New York less than two weeks ago, and Christopher had gotten tickets for the play already. She scanned the beautifully appointed room with its two double beds, elegant spreads and drapes, the view of Times Square. When they'd checked in, they'd discovered Christopher's secretary had only reserved one room, not two. And the hotel was completely booked due to a professional conference. Her husband had looked at her and said, "You can trust me." She'd believed him. And then to his chagrin, she'd made sure that they, indeed, did have two double beds...instead of one king-sized which would have been out of the question.

As it was, she wasn't as concerned about Christopher's desire as her own. She believed he'd keep his word...and stay in his bed. But she was terrifically susceptible to the sparks of desire in his eyes, let alone his kiss and touch.

Answering his question, she said again, "This is fine. We really don't have time to search for another hotel with two vacant rooms if we want to make the show before the curtain goes up."

"You can trust me, Jenny," he repeated as if he sensed she needed reassurance.

"I know I can. I'm more concerned about getting swept into something before I'm ready. Sharing a room is...intimate."

"So is being husband and wife."

"That's exactly what I mean, Christopher. You see us that way. I don't. Not yet." As he approached her, she felt the ever-present pull toward him and thought about scurrying away. But she knew she had to stand her ground.

"I'll tell you what," he said gently. "If you wake up in the morning wanting a room of your own, we'll find one for you tomorrow night. Here or wherever we have to go."

The tender feelings she couldn't deny urged her to ask, "Have you always been this good to me?"

There was a change in his eyes, and she couldn't read the emotion. But then he smiled and said, "Let's just think about now. Since we won't have time for dinner, I'll order something from room service we can pick at while we're dressing. We can go to a restaurant after the play.''

A night on the town with Christopher. It sounded wonderful. During the past week and a half, they'd spent many hours together. He'd taken her to the doctor again, and Dr. Coswell had said she could drive or ride. They'd bought the vehicle Jenny liked so much so she could get around herself, taking care of details for the auction that was now only two weeks away. They'd also walked, talked, even gone antiquing. Christopher had seemed to enjoy the time as much as she had. Always, there was the electricity between them that crackled whenever they got within a foot of each other. It was a teasing excitement that just made her want to spend even more time with him to explore it.

His good-night kisses courted her, and if kisses could persuade, she would have invited him into their bed days ago. But something more elusive than conscious held her back. She'd have to be careful tonight or having two double beds in the room would be irrelevant.

After Jenny disappeared around the corner to the dressing area and bathroom, Christopher let the guilt he'd been holding at bay sweep over him.

Have you always been this good to me?

If she counted material possessions, he'd always been very good to her. But he strongly suspected material wealth didn't mean much to this Jenny, and he was beginning to think it didn't to the old Jenny, either. Unfortunately he'd never realized that. He'd never realized a lot of things.

When he called room service, he ordered a club sandwich, a fruit plate, and a piece of quiche. Jenny used to love quiche. As he hung up, he heard the shower running. It *was* intimate sharing a room with her. So intimate he could vividly picture her under that shower, her hair streaming wet, her body glistening...

Whoa, boy. You told her she could trust you.

With a low groan, he strode to the window and stared down at the taxis and limousines and the countless pedestrians that made Times Square on a Friday night a street fair. He must have concentrated so well that time actually passed. Room service knocked at the door. He answered it, glad for something to do.

He'd signed for the food, tipped the waiter, and closed the door behind him, when Jenny came around the corner. The vision she presented knocked the air from his lungs. He remembered the sequined top that looked like mother-of-pearl shining rainbows in the sunlight. Even the narrow straps bore sequins. The skirt was full, a soft white fabric that fell to her knees. Her white high heels made her legs look longer, beautifully curved. His heart sped so fast he didn't think the rhythm would ever be normal again.

"I thought I'd wait and put on my lipstick after we eat." Her voice was soft and unsure, as if she thought he was staring because something was wrong with her appearance.

"You don't *need* lipstick," he responded, his voice husky.

She smiled. "What a nice compliment."

She thought he was being *nice?* "You wore that dress on our honeymoon."

"Oh."

So soft...her voice...her skin...the skirt of that dress. He remembered as if it was yesterday, and his body grew rigid with the need that had aroused him then and aroused him now. Neither he nor Jenny breathed.

She blinked first, took a tremulous breath, and then went to the table where the waiter had set their food. "Let's see what we have."

He knew exactly what they had. Enough chemistry between them to blow up the damned hotel! "You go ahead

and get started,'' he said in a voice he barely recognized
as his own. ''I'm going to take a quick shower.''

Quick and *very* cold.

Horns tooted, cars backfired, the spring breeze caught the
fringes of Jenny's white shawl as well as tendrils of hair
along her cheeks. Other theatergoers brushed past them,
some dressed casually, others more elegantly. Christopher
heard and saw it all in a haze because he was preoccupied
with watching his wife, with worrying about whether the
play would bring back memories for her and exactly what
they'd be.

After they entered the theater and the usher showed them
to their seats, Jenny canvassed the rows of seats and the
stage, letting her eyes linger on the side balconies. He
watched her closely, but when she'd finished looking
around, she gave a small shrug and laid her hand on top of
his on the armrest.

Glad she felt comfortable touching him, wishing she felt
a lot more comfortable, he didn't move—hoping she'd keep
her hand there, no matter what did or didn't happen during
the play. When the music started, he glanced at her, but
she was gazing at the stage.

During the first act she barely moved. During the second
she shifted in her seat. Her hand grew cold on top of his.
At the last song before intermission, tears slipped down her
cheeks. When the lights came on, he leaned close to her.
''Are you all right?''

''Can we go to the lobby? I need some...air.''

Concerned, he took her arm as they walked up the red-
carpeted aisle and found an empty space near the ticket
window.

''The music is so beautiful. But it makes me feel so

sad," she explained. "It's a sadness that extends beyond the play...right into my heart. I don't understand it."

He stroked her cheek. "Maybe it's just a response to everything that's happened the past few weeks."

"I don't know. Something just feels so...wrong."

Not wanting to rush going back inside, he asked, "Would you like something to drink?"

"A soda would be great."

"I'll be right back."

During the second half of the play, Jenny didn't put her hand on Christopher's. In fact she seemed to move away from him in body and in spirit. When an emotional song played at the climax of the production, her shoulders shook and he knew she was crying. Draping his arm around her, he pulled her close to him. As the actors took their third curtain call, she tugged away and blew her nose.

Since they were practically in the center of the row, no one shoved by them. Christopher said, "I know a little place where we can get coffee and something to eat. It's within walking distance if you can manage in those shoes."

She stuffed the tissue in her purse. "I've been wearing heels since I was twelve. I'll be fine."

Since her accident, he'd learned more about his wife's strength than in the five years he'd known her.

Christopher tucked Jenny's hand through the crook of his elbow as they walked in silence, taking in the smells, sights, and sounds of New York. The streets were filled with people at eleven-thirty at night.

They walked about five blocks until Christopher stopped and opened a heavy glass door. After the hostess showed them to a glass-topped table for two with a collage of play-bills under the glass, he took both of Jenny's hands in his. "Any more flashes?"

She shook her head. "The theater felt familiar. Like déjà

vu. As if I'd been there before. But nothing specific. Did I cry like that the last time we were here?''

Christopher's gut tightened, and it had nothing to do with hunger. ''Why do you ask?''

With a shrug she said, ''I'm just trying to figure this all out.''

''I don't know if you cried when you first saw the play. I wasn't with you.''

Her eyes widened and still glistened from her tears. ''I don't understand. When I asked if we could come again, you led me to believe we'd been here together! Why didn't you tell me?''

''I *am* telling you.''

''Why now? Why not before? What's going on, Christopher?''

Where at first she'd been confused, now he saw the sparks in her eyes and heard the note in her voice that told him she was angry. ''I thought it would be better for you if you remembered on your own.''

''It seems as if I did a lot more on my own than I imagined.'' She slid her hands away from his and sat straight in the wrought iron chair.

''You didn't come to New York alone. You were with my mother.''

''Your mother? Why didn't you say so? Why didn't *she* tell me? I mentioned we were coming, seeing the same play... Did you tell her to lie to me?''

He sat back, remaining calm. Just as he did in his boardroom. ''She didn't lie.''

Jenny made a sound of protest. ''She just didn't tell me the truth. Like you. I could have asked her to come with me, to make it the same, to help me remember. You didn't give me that chance. What *aren't* you telling me now?''

He kept his eyes on hers. ''We were supposed to come together. But at the last minute, an associate from Boston flew in, and I had two days of meetings and conference calls.''

"And I was terribly disappointed so you asked your mother to come along with me."

"You remember?"

"No. But I'd bet it wasn't the first time it happened."

The edge on her words made him defensive. "We came here together about a year after we were married and had a great weekend."

Standing, she tossed her shawl over her arm and picked up her purse. "I'm sure it was a darn sight better weekend than we're going to have this time. I've lost my appetite. I'll see you back at the hotel."

With a scrape of his chair, he was on his feet and clasping her arm. "Oh, no, you won't. You're not walking the streets of New York by yourself."

"I don't intend to walk them. I'll get a cab."

"They don't like to drive a few blocks."

"I'll tip very well," she tossed at him as she yanked away, left the table, and headed for the door.

Christopher stared after her for a few moments then caught up with her at the glass door. He put his hand on it to keep her from opening it. "We'll go back together."

Defiance flashed in her eyes and her expression seemed to say, "All right. You've proven you're stronger. I'll do what you say. But I don't have to like it."

Christopher had heard about the silent treatment. He'd never experienced it. Jenny had been quiet in the past. But she'd never pursed her lips as if she were biting her tongue and refused to speak to him. But he didn't try to talk to her or touch her as they walked back, knowing she'd rebuff him.

Rebuffed.

Is that how she'd felt when he didn't come home until

after she was asleep? When he put golf dates and business appointments before their plans?

He was beginning to see why she'd slipped away from him; he wasn't sure how to win her back. And if she ever did remember the man who'd given her the attention she'd needed...

He felt entrapped in a cage of his own making. Possibly he could repair the damage and hope the present could transform the past. But that might be a pipe dream.

The elevator was crowded as they stepped on. When it stopped at the third floor and more guests piled in, Jenny stood in front of him. If he bent his head, her hair would touch his nose. He could smell her shampoo...smell her perfume...smell her. At the fifth floor, another couple wedged themselves in. Jenny's body tensed as she had to back up another pace. Her shoulders pressed against his chest, and he blew out a breath instead of wrapping his arms around her and pressing her even closer so she'd know exactly how much he wanted her.

As the elevator stopped at the tenth floor and a few people dribbled out, Jenny stepped forward. When they exited on the twenty-third floor, her cheeks were flushed. But he didn't know if that was from anger or from the proximity they'd been forced to maintain.

After he unlocked their door, she avoided his gaze and went to the windows to close the drapes. "Do you want to get ready for bed first or should I?"

"Go ahead," he said. "I'll catch the late news."

Finished in ten minutes, she appeared in the room again in a cream satin gown and robe, her feet bare. He'd discarded his jacket, tie and shirt, and now held his sleeping shorts in his hand. When she caught sight of his bare chest, she stopped. As her gaze roamed from his shoulders, to his nipples almost hidden amidst the hair, then to the waistband of his trousers, his blood surged harder and faster. Heat filled the room and the low drone of the television couldn't muffle the pounding of his heart.

She bit her lower lip. He wanted to kiss it, and her upper lip, and her neck...

Reminding himself he'd assured her she could trust him, realizing that after tonight she might not believe she could, he willed himself to turn away from her and think about brushing his teeth rather than burying himself inside of her. The transition was practically impossible.

When he emerged from the bathroom, she was already in the bed by the door, on the side by the door, with covers drawn up to her chin. Her robe lay at the foot of her bed.

Don't think about the way that nightgown looks on her body, he told himself as he pressed the remote to silence the TV and slid under the sheet. Then he switched off the bedside lamp, hoping the darkness would help lessen the tension. But it didn't. He could feel it as intensely as he had when she'd stared at his chest.

"Good night, Jenny."

"Good night," she returned softly without the snap he expected. But he should know by now his wife no longer did the expected.

Minutes seemed like hours as he tossed and turned, checking the clock, listening for signs of restlessness from Jenny but not hearing anything. The last thing he remembered was the clock's red digits at two-thirty until a noise from her bed awakened him.

"Christopher!"

Instantly alert, he flicked on the light. She was sitting up, her hair tousled, her eyes bright.

"I remember," she said breathlessly.

Christopher froze, and one question blared in his mind. Was his marriage over before he could revive it?

Chapter Seven

Christopher's blood pounded in his ears at her words. In a moment, he was up, sitting on her bed, facing her. "What do you remember?"

Jenny stared past him, looking at a picture in her mind. "Shopping. Your mother and I shopped at Bloomingdale's. She was trying a new perfume. I opened my purse to check my list. And there was this other piece of paper there. Folded. Like a letter. And when I looked at it, I felt so sad. So confused. I..."

Her breath hitched, her eyes glistened, and he could see the sadness and confusion. Taking her hand, he ran his thumb soothingly across her palm. "What was on the paper?"

She took her other hand up and over her forehead, brushing her bangs to the side. "I don't know. I can't see it. Why can't I see it?"

Christopher believed Jenny had amnesia. But more and more, he suspected the cause wasn't just the trauma of the accident. There was something she didn't want to remember. It was obvious in her lack of memories of *him*. Maybe she'd been filled with guilt over her affair and her mind was keeping all of it suppressed so she didn't have to face it.

"Christopher, there's something wrong. I can't put my finger on it. Do you know what it is?"

If he knew for sure, he'd be tempted to tell her and pull both of them out of this quagmire of doubts and tension. "I don't know, Jenny."

She searched his face, then folded her arm across herself as if she were cold, though she still let him hold her hand.

He saw a shiver ripple through her and goose bumps broke out on her arms. Despite what had passed between them earlier, he knew she needed him. He couldn't remember ever being so sure of anything. Usually he relied on words and logic, but this knowing was pure instinct.

When he let go of her hand and stood, he saw the disappointment on her face and wondered how many times in their marriage he'd missed it or ignored it. Before it could become another wall between them, he lifted her sheet and slid into the bed beside her, folding her into his arms. She didn't resist or pull away, and he stroked her hair as he had wanted to do so many times since she'd come home from the hospital.

As her body warmed against his, he could feel another heat starting that had no place in this bed tonight. Not if he wanted to win her trust. Not if he wanted to win her back. "Would you like me to hold you while you sleep?"

She tilted her head back against his shoulder. "That's not fair to you."

Fair. A word that was beginning to have a myriad of meanings for both of them. "Having you in my arms right now is what I need, too." He kissed her forehead and stroked her face with his knuckle, knowing it was so. Then he reached over to the light and switched it off. As he laid his head on the pillow and Jenny settled against his chest, he found new meaning in sharing a bed that had nothing to do with sex and everything to do with caring.

They breathed in unison and Christopher finally felt his body relax. Sleep came quickly and he embraced it, inhaling Jenny's scent, praying they could truly find each other again.

When Jenny awakened, she found herself curled intimately against Christopher, her hand on his chest, her knee over his thigh. She didn't move for a few minutes, feeling...familiarly comfortable. But not so familiar or comfortable that she could stay where she was. As she attempted to slide her knee from his leg, she felt his fingers move on her arm.

"Good morning," he said, his voice husky, his hair rumpled, his jaw dark from the night's growth of beard.

She scooted, then, at least six inches across the sheet. "I was just getting up..." When he clasped her arm, she stilled.

"You were enjoying being where you were...at least until you thought better of it," he concluded.

"I didn't want you to think..."

"That you were offering something you weren't? I told you, Jenny, you can trust me."

She *did* trust him. It was herself she didn't trust. "I felt safe last night...with you holding me. When I don't understand what I remember, what I feel, it seems everything spins. With your arms around me, it stops."

"Did you remember anything else?"

She shook her head. "No. And I need to know something. Why didn't you tell me before we came that the last time I was here it was with your mother?"

His hand slid from her arm, his jaw tensed, and his eyes became shuttered.

"Don't do that, Christopher."

With brows arched, he asked, "What?"

"You're closing me out as if I had no business trying to find the answer. You asked your mother to keep something from me, and I want to know why. Don't tell me it was because of Dr. Coswell's advice, either."

Grimacing, he pushed himself up against the headboard. "You're something, you know that?"

"Excuse me?"

He blew out a breath. "If you had been like this before, I wonder if..." Stopping abruptly, he looked her in the eye. "I didn't tell you out of self-preservation. Or marriage preservation. Or maybe just plain ego. In the fall when it happened...when I had to cancel, you didn't make a big deal of it, and I didn't want to admit to myself how disappointed you were. And now, something made me believe you would be very disappointed all over again."

"You were trying to protect me?"

"I think I was trying to protect the closeness growing stronger between us. I didn't want to disrupt it until I absolutely had to."

"Oh, Christopher." Her heart filled with all the tenderness that had been brewing since the day he'd brought her home and maybe even more than that because it seemed to overflow her heart's boundaries. Could she have fallen in love with him again so quickly? That would take some thinking about.

"Do you want to check out and go home?" he asked.

Maybe what they both needed was time away from home where she didn't expect to remember, where they could just be a man and a woman getting to know each other again.

"I think I'd rather take a buggy ride through Central Park. And maybe go to the top of the Empire State Building."

"I hope with me," he said with a slow smile that made him look altogether too male and sexy for her peace of mind.

But she was feeling reckless this morning, intrigued by this man she felt so drawn to, still mindful of how she'd felt sleeping in his arms. "Definitely with you," she answered, wanting to kiss him but holding back until she sorted out her feelings.

He slid his feet over the side of the bed. "Bagels and coffee first?"

She nodded, looking forward to spending the day and another night with her husband.

Dinner with Christopher in a revolving restaurant high atop a New York City hotel was the proverbial cherry on a day that couldn't have been more perfect. They'd acted like tourists, enjoying every minute. At least Jenny had and Christopher had appeared to have fun, too. He'd caught her hand as they'd run across streets and placed his protectively at the small of her back as he guided her through crowds. Each touch, each companionable brushing of arms, elbows or knees quickened her breath and warned her that they were long past strangers and could never just be friends. As Christopher's gaze met hers over coffee and the last bite of dessert late in the evening, there was a light in his eyes that had been banked all day. Now it sparkled clearly and she knew she'd have to deal with it.

"Are you ready to leave?" he asked. "We could take another buggy ride…"

"No. Let's go back to the room."

His eyes held a question, but she wasn't yet sure of the answer.

The skyscrapers and streetlights blocked any illusion of stars or sky. The earth seemed to be created of pavement, curbs, hurried people, taxis and traffic lights—a universe unto itself that was noisy and exciting, exotic and dilapidated all at the same time. But in the midst of it, Jenny was more aware of the man walking beside her than of the sights or sounds of Times Square. His charcoal suit coat lay perfectly across his broad shoulders, his trousers—superbly tailored and creased, gently brushed the tops of his black wing-tipped shoes. As he pushed back his jacket to drop one hand casually into his pocket, she remembered his long lean body against hers last night.

The doorman nodded to her and opened the glass door as they walked up to the entrance of their hotel.

Christopher took a deep breath as he let Jenny precede him through the door, knowing he had to take his signals from her. She'd worn the same dress to dinner that she'd worn to his parents' party, adding her shawl to protect her from the night chill. But the dress still drove him crazy. That damn hole in the back. He could see her skin even through the shawl. And the way she walked, the feminine sway of her hips in high heels...

As they waited for the elevator, he knew he couldn't sleep in the same room with her tonight, not wanting to touch her in more than a comforting way. It was an issue he had to confront without upsetting her, without attempting to seduce her. The high-speed elevator whizzed them to the twenty-third floor. Jenny didn't glance at him once, and he wondered what she was thinking. She'd probably suggested they come back to the hotel because she was tired. She looked so beautiful...so vibrant...he'd forgotten she'd been in a coma a few weeks ago.

Jenny slipped off her shawl as they moved toward their room. In the swirl of fringe, her perfume rose up to him, stronger and more potent than earlier in the evening. The heat of her body intensified it, mingled with it, making his hold on his desire tenuous. Trying to ignore the adrenaline rushing through him, he unlocked the door. When he held it open and Jenny's shoulder brushed his chest as she passed him, he knew this could easily be the most difficult night of his life.

No, that wasn't true.

The night he hadn't known if she'd live or die had been the most difficult night of his life. This was just going to be...

When the door closed, he didn't move away. "Jenny."

She turned to face him.

"I'm going to get another room." For a moment he thought she might ask why. But when she started toward him and he gazed into her eyes, he knew that she knew why.

"They said they were booked to capacity."

"That was last night. Surely someone checked out."

"What if they don't have a room? Will you move to a different hotel? Is distance going to help?"

The whole situation, his doubts, the sheer sexual frustration, made him swear. Then he raked his hand through his hair. "No. Distance isn't going to help. It won't take the wanting away. In spite of—" He stopped short. "I want you, Jenny. The more I'm around you, the more I want to kiss you and touch you and..."

He thought she'd stop a few feet away. He never expected her to stand so close, her chin tilted up, her voice so soft it was almost a whisper.

"I don't want you to get another room."

Keeping his hands at his sides so he wouldn't touch her and lose all control, he asked, "Are you afraid to stay here by yourself?"

Her eyes were as blue as a summer sky, as intent as he'd ever seen them. "No. I'm not afraid. But I need you here with me...in my bed."

"I can't hold you like last night and not—"

"I want you to make love to me."

Had Jenny ever said those words to him before? Certainly he would have remembered. Because there was no way he could ever forget his body's instantaneous response, or the aching in his heart so great his breath wouldn't leave his chest. But in the heartbeat of control vying with desire, he managed to ask, "Are you sure?"

"I'm sure." And in case he didn't believe her, she brought her hand to his face and stroked his jaw.

It was her scent, her touch, the certainty in her voice that made need more pressing than words, a kiss the beginning of a journey to the stars. Forcing himself to hold on to desire tightly, reminding himself Jenny remembered nothing about their physical relationship, he kissed her instead of carrying her to the bed, then he laced his hands in her hair rather than pressing her into his body where he needed her to be.

The kiss was everything he couldn't say about need, and touch and marriage and desire. He opened his mouth over hers, creating intimacy between them as much as he craved her hands on him. When her tongue tentatively slid along his lower lip, he groaned, praying he could hold on, hoping he could give her so much pleasure she'd never ever think about leaving him again. He stroked his tongue against hers, played, then thrust into her mouth until she moaned, dropped her purse and shawl to the floor, and slid her hands under his arms around his back, holding on tight. Breaking the kiss for breath, stilling his heart before it leapt from his chest, he cradled her head in his hands and gazed into her eyes. Their blue depths were filled with silver light as magical as a star's.

"Jenny, I know you don't remember what it was like between us. I don't want to do anything to scare you or…"

"I'm not in the least bit worried about you scaring me," she said with a small smile.

He kissed the smile, the corner of her mouth, her neck until she arched toward him, murmuring his name. When he took her earlobe between his lips and laved it, he felt the quiver in her body that he knew so well. His fingertips played on the skin her dress left bare. Her shivers told him she was ready for more than kisses.

Bringing his hands to the back of her dress, he unfastened the hooks and slid down the short zipper. With a nudge, the material fell forward. The bra she'd told him about was a slightly lighter blue than the dress, sheer and silky.

"That bra could drive a man crazy," he admitted, his voice hoarse.

"Then maybe I should take it off," she suggested, her hands going to the hook at her neck.

He'd taken pleasure from her body during their marriage. But he didn't know if he'd ever looked at her like this or needed her so much. He shucked off his suit coat, dropping it to the floor on top of her shawl. Then he tugged off his tie and tore at the buttons of his shirt as if they were enemies that needed to be conquered. Once he was barechested, he traced his thumbs down her neck and over her shoulders, wanting to touch everything at once, needing to wrap himself in her.

Jenny didn't know if she was being forward or wifely or simply wanton. But Christopher was creating a need in her so great that her desire for him, this new love, urged her to respond freely and to give him the same pleasure he was giving her. She reached out, sliding her hands upward from his belt, up through the tawny hair on his chest. When he sucked in a breath, she knew she was doing something right.

Her hands went to his belt, and he caught them. "I want this to be so special for you that..."

She saw him searching for a way to say it. "That I'll remember?" Working the leather, she gazed into his eyes and said, "This will be special whether I remember or not."

"That's not what I was going to say." His voice was deep. "I want it to be so special that it doesn't *matter* whether you remember or not."

His expression and the emotion in his eyes told her he wanted this to be a new beginning for them. She wanted that, too, yet she sensed there was something very unfinished about their past. She could let those doubts interfere, or she could allow the moment to lead her.

She went with the moment and after she unfastened his belt, he lifted her in his arms and carried her to the bed. He laid her down, then quickly undressed and came down beside her. As she stared at him, he didn't move, just let her absorb everything about him she'd once known.

He had a magnificent body—textured, masculine, hard, filled with a strength she'd felt many times. But it was the hint of uncertainty in his gaze that led her to stroke her hand from his shoulder to his elbow.

He closed his eyes for a moment, and when he opened them again, he said, "You're still half dressed. I think we should do something about that."

She thought she'd help him, but she sighed and enjoyed his touch more than she managed to help. He seemed to appreciate her reactions, and when he'd finished, he gathered her in his arms and held her close. Her heart beat in unison with his—steady, then quicker and faster and harder. Time stopped as their need became palpable and Christopher's pulsing desire told her his restraint most surely would soon come to an end.

But she was wrong. He slowly kissed her, stroked her, and touched her until his name became a plea for fulfillment. Gently, he pushed away and she was confused for an instant. "Christopher, what's wrong? Did I..."

"Protection," he explained, a husky tremor in his voice. "It's in the drawer."

Protection. They hadn't talked about children—whether they'd wanted them in the past, whether they wanted them now. Of course, he was right to use it. Until they were more certain what the future would hold.

He came back to her, and she opened her arms to him, welcoming his passion, inviting him into her heart. He was her husband, and she wanted to know him in this—the most intimate way possible.

Holding himself up on his elbows, he kissed her with the sweetness of a first union, with the hunger of a man who had been deprived too long.

She raised her knees and when he ended the kiss, breaking to look into her eyes, she said, "I want you, Christopher."

"Those words are more arousing than your touch," he rasped and held himself at her entrance.

"I can touch, too," she reminded him and passed her hands down his back and over his buttocks to signal exactly what she wanted.

"Oh, Jenny. I can't wait any longer." He slid into her, giving her himself, filling an emptiness she hadn't even realized was there.

Unable to catch any of the words racing through her mind, she resisted the effort and gave herself up to the pure sensations of being loved by her husband. Being loved. He'd never said it. But surely…

As he retreated slightly, then thrust again, pleasure after erotic pleasure began building, heating, winding, until she clutched his shoulders and held on, lest she be swept away when the wave hit. Because she knew it would be tidal in proportion.

He whispered her on, murmured her name, let his breath mingle with hers in a deep, deep kiss. Then he brought one hand between their bodies, and she exploded with a moan, digging her fingers into his hair.

Their passion glistened on their skin as he rocked into her orgasm and found his own release. She held him, and he held her as they gulped in air, kissed each other's necks, then finally smiled as their hearts slowed to a more normal rhythm.

"What are you thinking?" he asked as he rolled to his side, taking her with him.

"I'm thinking we're wonderful together." She wanted to ask if they'd always been this way, but she remembered what he'd said about a new beginning, so instead of asking, she kissed him.

His response told her she was going to enjoy how wonderful they were together all over again.

The sun shone brightly on Sunday as they returned home. At the door, Christopher dropped their luggage and scooped Jenny up into his arms.

She laughed up at him, breathless, and held on tight. "What are you doing?"

"Carrying you over the threshold," he said simply, gently setting her down in the foyer and giving her a kiss that curled her toes.

No matter what their marriage had been before, they'd

started it over yesterday. When Christopher had made love to her last night...this morning...she'd known they belonged together. Only one thing could have made it more perfect—Christopher actually saying he loved her. Maybe as they grew closer, the words would follow the feelings and their combustible chemistry. She hadn't said them, either.

Because she sensed the way wasn't clear for them? Because she still felt a guardedness in him? That couldn't be. Not after the way they'd made love.

As his tongue swept her mouth, creating an emotional and physical craving for him all over again, she let the doubts fade and...

"Oh! I'm sorry," an unexpected voice said. "I just wanted to see if you needed anything."

Christopher lifted his head and grinned ruefully. "It's all right, Pauline." He kept his arm around Jenny. "I don't think we'll be needing anything else today."

"But, sir, I had Friday afternoon off and yesterday..."

"Go get Fred and take a drive or something. It's a beautiful day."

The housekeeper smiled at him. "I can see that. There's a casserole in the fridge for supper and there's a plate of cold cuts and another of fruit if you'd like something now. Oh, and Mrs. Langston has a message on her machine. It came in this morning. I knew you were on your way home or I would have called you with it."

"Is it anything urgent?" Jenny asked. She couldn't imagine who might have called unless it was Dave Hedgewick wanting to talk to her about her photographs.

"I'm not sure." Pauline's expression was neutral. "I think Fred and I might take that drive. I'll see you both in the morning." And with that, she disappeared into the kitchen, discreetly leaving them alone.

Jenny laughed and looked up at her husband. "I think she believes we need some privacy." The laughter faded from her lips as she saw Christopher's serious expression. "What's wrong?"

"I think you should go listen to your message."

"It might just be Dave wanting to discuss the gallery showing."

Christopher gave a shrug. "Then let's go see. Afterward we can try out that sofa in your sitting room. We've never undressed each other there before."

The words were right, in sync with the mood they'd returned with. But his smile was forced, and she felt a tension that hadn't been there before. She was beginning to know Christopher quite well. Until they listened to the message, he wouldn't relax.

They went through the kitchen and descended the steps in silence. As she crossed her office, he followed her. She pressed the play button on the machine.

"Jenny, it's Marty. I've been worried. You said you'd call me after you got back and you didn't. I've tried you a few times, but you didn't answer and I know your situation. Please just let me know what's happening."

The man's voice sounded very concerned, and she didn't know what to make of it.

When she looked up at her husband, he asked in a curt tone, "Who's Marty?"

Chapter Eight

Jenny's heart raced. She knew anger when she heard it, but she didn't know what had caused it. "I don't know who Marty is. I've only seen the name once before..."

"Where?"

Her husband's sharpness hurt. "Christopher, what's wrong? Why are you being so—"

He clasped her wrist and his eyes bored into her. "I want to know where you've seen his name."

"On a slip of paper between some bills in my wallet."

"I looked through your wallet and didn't find anything."

Pulling her hand from his grasp, she asked, "Why were you going through my wallet?"

"It was after your accident. I was trying to find out where you'd been. What else was on the paper? A last name? An address?"

"Just the name Marty and the numbers 6/8."

"And you have no idea what it means?"

"No! And I don't appreciate—"

"Was it your handwriting or someone else's?"

"Mine. And that's the last question I'm going to answer until you tell me why you're interrogating me as if I'm a criminal."

"There's nothing to tell," he snapped, glancing at the answering machine. "I want you to get me that slip of paper."

"No."

He looked as if she'd slapped him. "Jenny—"

"Tell me why you're so angry."

His silence was worse than his sharp tone.

"Christopher, tell me *something*."

It was as if he'd turned to stone in front of her eyes. She was afraid to pursue this, but she knew she had to. "Didn't last night mean anything to you?"

"You have no idea."

His neutrality sparked her temper. "No, I don't. I also don't know a man named Marty or why I was in an accident near Binghamton. You told me you didn't know what I was doing there. I assumed I had gone shopping or was there to do something in connection with one of the charities. But now I wonder. Why didn't you or anyone else know where I'd gone? How long was I gone?"

"Four days."

His voice was so dispassionate that the tone frightened her more than his anger. She thought back to his attitude after she'd awakened from her coma...when she'd come home. The distance between them. She'd thought he was merely giving her some space...not pushing her. But what if that distance had been there for a long time? What if...?

It all coalesced into a recognizable picture, like a photograph developing. The suspicions, the doubts and questions, Luke's wariness... "You think I had an affair!"

Still he was silent.

"Tell me," she almost shouted.

"Dr. Coswell said—"

"I don't care what Dr. Coswell said. This is *my* life that's shredded to bits, not hers. Does she know about this?"

"I asked her advice. As I told you, as *she* told you, she said it would be better if you remember on your own."

"But I *don't* remember. Help me, Christopher."

"Help you? I've been trying to help you, Jenny, taking each day as it came while my doubts were killing me. Do you have any idea what it was like to come home one night to find a note that you'd left with no explanation but a plea for my understanding? Do you realize what it felt like to sit by your bed while you were in a coma wondering every minute where you'd been, who you'd been with, and not knowing if you'd live through it to tell me why?"

The air crackled with his anger and resentment, yet the pain of betrayal was there, too. As if he couldn't stand to look at her a moment longer, he turned away and started for the doorway.

She hurried after him and clasped his arm. "Christopher…"

He shook his head. "Until you remember, we'll never know. Last night I thought it would be best if you never did remember—so we could start over. But I was deluding myself. This will always be between us. And I don't know if I can live with it."

As he pulled away and went upstairs, she knew she had to let him go. At least for now. She had a lot of thinking to do.

And a search to undertake.

Surely, if she'd had an affair, there'd be evidence of something…somewhere. A memento. A note. A picture. A letter. Something other than Christopher's suspicions and a strange man's voice on an answering machine.

Who could the man be?

And why would her husband think she was having an affair?

After last night...

If the passion between her and Christopher in their years together had neared the intensity of last night, she couldn't envision ever *wanting* to make love with someone else. Granted, she didn't remember the last five years since she'd met Christopher. She couldn't be sure of the person she'd become. But she knew her heart. She couldn't imagine marrying him for any other reason than love. Terrific physical attraction wouldn't have been enough. And if she loved him deeply enough to marry him, to want to spend her life with him, she couldn't have cheated on him. She couldn't have betrayed him.

Apparently Christopher had a different image of her. She had to find out why.

With great care, she searched her desk—every drawer, every pigeonhole, every crevice. She went through her file cabinet looking for clues, finding only forms, copies of grants, reminders. Nothing personal. Nothing that would lead her to the truth.

When she'd turned her office upside down, she went to the attic to the box that held her mother's papers without really knowing why, just hoping maybe there was some link to her trip to Binghamton or wherever she'd gone. But she only found cards and letters that didn't tell her anything. When she decided to find her husband again, to hash out whatever had happened between them, he was gone. So was his car. She guessed he'd gone to work, to his refuge, to the place where he felt safe from the pain he thought she'd inflicted.

She couldn't know for sure if she'd betrayed him or not.

But her own self-knowledge told her she'd rip her heart out first.

Now, how could she get Christopher to believe her?

When Christopher answered his private line on Monday afternoon, he expected to hear Luke, Jud or his parents. Instead, after his usual greeting, he heard Jenny's voice.

"I'm sorry to bother you, Christopher, but I wanted to know if you'd be coming home for supper tonight."

He'd left yesterday afternoon and hadn't been back. "I'm not sure."

"Did you come home at all last night?"

Her voice wasn't accusing. It was...resigned. "No. I had calls to make."

"Did you get any sleep?"

Certain her concern was sincere, it almost pained him. Anything about her did. "Some. I have a couch in my office."

"You can't avoid me forever," she said softly.

"Jenny—"

"We have to talk. It's the only way we'll work out the problems we had...or have. Please come home."

He remembered the feel of her in his arms, their passion-rich night when he'd mistakenly thought he could put the past *in* the past. "All right. I'll be home around six."

"I won't keep you then. Have a good afternoon."

Her gentle goodbye stayed with him throughout the day.

When Christopher came home a few minutes before six, he went upstairs to change clothes. He didn't see Jenny on the way. The door to the master suite stood open. As he looked inside, he realized how difficult it would be to look into her blue eyes and not let her see his pain. If she knew how she'd hurt him, how she could still hurt him, it would make him vulnerable to her, to feelings he didn't know if he should harbor.

Now, he wanted her to get her memory back. He wanted to look into the face of more than a shadow and decide

what to do. After changing into jeans and a T-shirt, thinking
a ride after supper was the healthiest thing for him to do,
he went downstairs to the dining room. Instead of Pauline
bustling about, he found Jenny, adjusting a platter of
chicken breasts in some type of sauce on a silver trivet.
She, too, was wearing jeans and a knit top but her pink
shirt sported a streak of flour.

Her cheeks were flushed as she said, "I gave Pauline the
afternoon and evening off. I thought we'd like to be alone."

Spending the evening alone with her. He wished it were
that simple. "You cooked?"

"Yep. Chicken dijon, fresh broccoli, parsley potatoes
and lemon meringue pie. Though the meringue looks a little…wilted."

She'd gone to a lot of trouble. In fact… "You've never
cooked us dinner before."

"Then it's long past time I did."

"Jenny…"

"Go ahead and sit. I'll get the rest."

When she returned, he'd poured two glasses of water
from the pitcher on the table. She'd used her mother's china
and crystal.

She fixed two plates and set one before him. It felt funny
to have her serve him. It made him uncomfortable. But she
looked a helluva lot more relaxed than he felt.

"Tell me about your day," she said reaching for her
water.

He fingered his fork. "Do you really want to make small
talk?"

"I want to have a conversation with you and a good meal
before we get into anything heavy. Go ahead and taste it."

Come to think of it, he'd had nothing but coffee and a
few pastries that someone had brought in to his office since
yesterday when they'd returned. He was hungry, and the

aromatic smells tempted him almost as much as his wife did.

He tried a bite of the chicken and savored it. "It's very good."

"Thank you," she said with a smile, trying to set a course for the meal.

Okay, if that's what she wanted. He didn't need his stomach tied up in knots while they ate.

They managed a strained conversation about the upcoming auction and some of the items Jenny had seen, tagged and sorted. He asked if her photographs were ready for the showing on Saturday, and she told him she was driving into the gallery on Wednesday morning to talk with Dave Hedgewick about placement of the pictures.

They ate their slices of pie in silence. Finally Jenny poured two coffees. "Yesterday afternoon and evening I went through my office and our bedroom from top to bottom."

"What were you looking for?"

"Anything that would help us. I didn't find a clue as to who Marty is or why I was in Binghamton or anywhere in that area. I even looked through receipts—"

"I don't think a receipt will help with this."

"What will? Besides me getting my memory back?"

"I don't know."

Jenny knew the lack of words between them was too harmful, too overpowering to let last. "I need answers as much as you do, Christopher. Maybe even more. I have to find out what kind of woman I am. Because of the way I grew up, seeing the love between my mother and father, knowing the values they nourished and I've embraced, I don't believe I would ever be unfaithful to my husband."

She saw the emotion in Christopher's eyes chased away

quickly by the doubts that had found a home with him. "But you don't know for sure, do you?" he asked curtly.

How could she explain to him that knowing went far beyond surface facts or memory? Yet his suspicions must have grounds, too. "Tell me why you believe I was."

He pushed back his pie dish with a little shove. "You became quieter, distracted, evasive, as if you didn't want me anywhere near your thoughts. If you were on the phone and I came into the room, you quickly hung up. There were hang-up calls when I answered. You left me a note, saying you were going away for a few days, asking me to understand. No mention of when you'd be back. *If* you were coming back. And then your accident in a place where you had no good reason to be." He shook his head. "Since you've been home, there was another hang-up. And with that message yesterday... Granted, it all might be circumstantial, but the evidence points to your involvement with another man."

He said it coldly, like a judge pronouncing a sentence, like he'd already convicted her. "Why are you so willing to believe I'd do that to you? What makes you so sure I'd want to *have* an affair?"

His brown eyes were hard, his voice brusque. "Some women think the grass is always greener."

There was some element here she wasn't seeing. Why was he so ready to believe she'd be unfaithful? Just because of the signs? If she had looked for something from another man, *why* had she? "I'm not *some* woman, Christopher. If I turned to someone else, if our marriage was crumbling, then weren't we both to blame?"

Anger creased his brows and tensed his jaw as he pushed back his chair. "I never contemplated sleeping in the arms of another woman. I made vows and I believed in them. But now I'm not so sure you did." As he stood, he said,

"This isn't getting us anywhere. I'm going riding. Leave the dishes. Pauline will clean them up in the morning."

He avoided her gaze as he closed the subject and made it clear that if their marriage hadn't been in trouble before, it certainly was now. When he left the dining room, she had no idea what to do next.

Tears came to her eyes and she realized she truly loved Christopher, whether it had happened since her accident or whether the love had abided in her heart from before. She wanted to fight for this marriage, but she wasn't sure how. She needed advice and she didn't know who to turn to. It had to be someone who knew Christopher, who knew about his suspicions and the accident.

Luke immediately came to mind. Yet she hesitated. Knowing what she knew now, she suspected Luke had doubts about her as well. Suddenly she remembered her conversations with Jud, his openness to her. Maybe he could help.

Going to her office, she found the Star Four's number on her Rolodex where she'd seen it earlier. Before she lost her courage, she dialed. The housekeeper answered. Jud was in the office in the barn. Jenny could wait for him to return her call or try out there. She jotted down the number, pushed the button on the phone and dialed again.

"Star Four," a man answered in a deep voice.

"Jud?"

"Yes. And who...Jenny, is that you?"

"None other. Do you have a few minutes?"

"Sure. Is something wrong?"

She didn't quite know how to start. "I...uh...do you know that Christopher thinks I had an affair?"

After a long pause, Jud answered. "That's what he told me. Did you remember?"

"No. Nothing about him and me. And he has all these reasons he thinks he's right."

"How about you? What do you think?"

"I can't believe I'd be capable of that deceit. Maybe I just don't want to believe it."

"His doubts are eating at him, Jenny."

"I can see that and I don't know what to do. He keeps walking away from me..."

Jud swore. "That's Christopher. When he's hurt or unsettled, he closes down, focuses on what's safe."

"Work."

"Usually," Jud agreed.

"What should I do? How do I reach him?"

"What do you want?"

"I want our marriage. But if he can't forgive something he thinks I did..."

"I'm not a marriage counselor, Jenny."

"No. But you're Christopher's close friend." Jud wasn't the type of man to meddle in other people's problems, and she knew she was probably putting him in a difficult position.

Finally he said, "If you really want to save your marriage, you've got to keep trying. When he walks away, go after him. If he won't listen, rope him and hog-tie him if you have to."

She had to smile. "He's a lot stronger than I am."

"You do it right, and you can match his strength any day."

Right. What would that be? Tie him with her love? She sighed. "Jud, I didn't mean to put you in the middle of this."

"You're not. I didn't tell you anything I wouldn't say in front of Christopher's nose."

"Thank you."

"I didn't do anything," he said gruffly.

"Yes, you did. You gave me hope."

When she hung up, she decided she *was* going to let the dishes sit. She had the sudden, overwhelming desire to see Wind Feather.

Best Chance nickered with Christopher's vigorous stroke of the brush.

"Sorry, boy." Before he rode Scout, he wanted to give the new horse some attention.

Attention.

Why would I want to have an affair? his wife had asked.

He blamed Jenny for the situation they were in and, Lord knows, he wanted to believe it was all her fault. Yet his thoughts went round and round. Guilt as much as anger had driven him from the dining room, and it was about time he admitted it. He couldn't help wondering if his inattentiveness to her had driven her into another man's arms.

It didn't excuse her but it made him look at his marriage differently. He'd always thought it was perfect. He worked, provided them with a beautiful home, anything they wanted, and thought he was meeting his goals, being successful, being a good husband. But now he had to rethink all of it. Readjusting his idea of life and work and relationships left him feeling terrifically off course and adrift, as if he had no compass to guide him. And his need and desire for Jenny, in spite of what she'd done, unnerved him more.

When the stable door opened, Christopher took the grooming brush over Best Chance again. Those light footsteps didn't belong to Fred. He kept brushing the horse's backside until Jenny stood next to him. She didn't say anything for a moment, and he breathed in her scent—shampoo, perfume and woman. His heart pounded and he wished to God it wouldn't.

"Will you teach me to ride?"

He turned to face her. "Now?"

"Yes."

"I was going to take Scout out."

"I can go with you," she suggested.

"I was going to give him his head, Jenny, and give him a good workout."

"Then I guess I'll just have to wait. Maybe tomorrow when you come home."

How many times had she wanted to spend time with him and he'd put her off? How many times had she waited for him and he'd been hours late? Should a past pattern make him feel guilty about his feelings now? He'd just needed some space, something physical to do.

She stood waiting for his answer without impatience, just with a determined assumption he would teach her sometime. That determination was a new quality about her, and he couldn't help but admire it. Just as he couldn't help but remember New York City and making love with her until he didn't know where he left off and she began.

"Fred can take Scout out tomorrow. Wait here. I'll get you a saddle."

To keep his mind off the shine on Jenny's hair, the snugness of her jeans, the smallness of her feet in the practically new boots she must have unearthed from her closet, he explained what he was doing as he cinched the girth under Wind Feather, slipped on the bridle, then tightened the girth again. When he led the horse outside, Jenny followed.

"I'm going to lengthen the stirrup so it's easier for you to mount. Or would you rather I give you a boost?"

"Teach me how to do it the right way."

Standing behind her, he said, "Put your left foot in the stirrup and take hold of the pommel while you pull yourself up."

She glanced at him over her shoulder. "As easy as making meringue."

He could lean down and kiss her half smile, he could lead her back into the stable, lay her down in the hay...

With an experimental hop, Jenny hoisted herself into the saddle.

Watching her face as she settled herself, her joy as she looked around, he realized how different she was now than when she'd tried riding at twenty-one. She'd been uncertain then...fearful. Now her mood was anticipatory and curious. Had her accident changed her so much? Or was he just looking at her differently?

"What do you think?" he asked, adjusting her stirrup.

"It's great. Like sitting on top of the world." She blushed. "Or at least on top of a small hill."

He had to smile. "Well, this hill moves. Let's go for a walk so you get the feel of her."

The leaves rustled with the evening breeze. Boughs sighed as Christopher stared straight ahead, soothed by the clomping of Wind Feather's hooves.

"Can I have the reins?"

He stopped and so did Wind Feather. "Are you sure?"

"I don't think walking her around the paddock is living too dangerously."

Adjusting the reins over the horse's head, he came alongside of Jenny. When she took the leather from him, their fingers brushed.

"Christopher?"

He could see in her eyes what was coming, and he didn't want to hash it out again. "Let's give it a rest for now. Okay?"

Biting her lower lip, she said, "All right. If you promise you'll come home tomorrow night and give me another lesson."

Mulling over the pros and cons, he finally decided giving her lessons couldn't hurt them and might help. Maybe if he taught her how to ride, he could pretend they were a normal couple. Maybe he could believe they still had a marriage.

Chapter Nine

The crisscross strips of satin on the neckline of Jenny's fuchsia dress emphasized the creaminess of her skin as she tilted her head and smiled at Dave Hedgewick. Christopher's gut tightened. It had been quite a night for her. Her photographs were a smash. Half of them had already sold. Men and women alike couldn't wait to meet her. The women he didn't mind. The men...

He kept wondering if one of them could be Marty. Every male looked at her in that slim dress as if they wanted her to belong to them. When another man in a navy suit walked up to her and tapped her shoulder, Christopher gritted his teeth.

"Why the scowl, Son? You should be proud of your wife. Tonight is a great accomplishment for her." His mother looked elegant in a beige dress with a matching jacket. But her expression was concerned.

"I know it is," he responded with a sigh. "And I *am* proud of her. I'm sorry Dad couldn't be here."

"I am, too. But he won't be back until tomorrow afternoon."

"Did anyone go with him?"

"No. He flew himself. I would have gone along, but he said his meetings were in a town with not much happening. No shopping. No shows. He still doesn't understand that just being with him would be enough for me."

"If he had meetings, he didn't want you to be bored."

"I suppose that's a man's way of looking at it. Not mine. How are you and Jenny doing? She said she enjoyed New York and remembered being there and shopping with me. I guess you were right to wait to tell her you didn't go there with her."

His mother was fishing, but he wasn't prepared to talk about his marriage. "I don't know if I was right. But she understood."

"So everything's all right between you?"

Everything was definitely *not* all right when a husband and wife slept in separate bedrooms.

They'd spent time together this past week every evening as he'd taught Jenny the basics of riding. Each night the lesson had lasted a little longer. Last night they'd ridden across the pastures to the bank of a stream and watched the sunset. He'd wanted to take her in his arms, kiss her, make love to her under the descending streams of sunlight. But they hadn't even dismounted, and he'd decided the space between them was safer than the pain of being too close.

His mother was waiting for an answer. "We're working on it, Mother."

"It's more than just the accident and her amnesia, isn't it?"

At that moment his pager went off. He took it from his inside jacket pocket and checked the number. "I have to make a call."

"I hope business isn't going to take you away from a night that's important to your wife."

A month ago it might have. But since then he'd delegated more responsibility to members of his workforce. "I won't let it."

After Christopher made a call on the cell phone in his car and answered a few of a new manager's questions, he returned to the gallery. Luke stepped away from a group discussing one of Jenny's photographs and crossed to Christopher. "Your wife's a hit. I don't even think she's had time for a glass of champagne."

"Maybe it's time I rectify that. That guy's been monopolizing her long enough."

"He's a reporter," Luke informed him.

"I don't care if he's the President of the United States," Christopher muttered as he snagged two champagne glasses from a tray and carried them to his wife.

When he offered one to her, she sent him a thank-you smile and introduced him to the reporter. But as soon as the man gave Christopher a short nod, he launched into another set of questions and didn't quit until Dave Hedgewick insisted Jenny join the other three showcased artists for group photographs for a rival newspaper. She flashed her husband an apologetic smile and let the gallery owner lead her away.

Luke must have seen his cousin's chagrin. He nudged his arm. "She's here to promote her work."

"I know that," Christopher snapped.

"Then you'd better smile so *she* knows you're not upset she can't stay by your side."

Christopher attempted a smile that was supposed to be encouraging, remembering all the cocktail parties, all the business dinners Jenny had attended with him when *he* was the one mingling, making contacts, negotiating in a less formal atmosphere than a boardroom. There again, she'd never complained. But what had she been thinking?

The night slipped by as Christopher stayed on the sidelines, watching Jenny, admiring her talent, wanting her. As all the customers and attendees finally dispersed, he waited for her in the front of the gallery where a few chairs had been positioned. She approached him, her satin purse in her hand, her smile brighter than a summer day.

"All set?" he asked, standing.

"In a minute. Dave insisted on giving me an accounting of my share of the profits on what we sold tonight. I don't think I've ever had a more exciting evening!"

Just as Christopher was about to tell her how radiant she looked, how proud he was of her, Hedgewick strode toward them.

The gallery owner handed her an envelope. "Congratulations. I have no doubts we'll sell the rest tomorrow. I'd like to plan another showing of your work late in the summer. Maybe a week-long exhibition. What do you think?"

"So soon?"

He grinned. "When you're hot, you're hot. Your photographs touch a basic emotional chord in anyone who looks at them. I'm just grateful I'm the one who found you." Taking her hand, he clasped it between his two. "Your talent is special, Jenny, and we're going to show it to as many people as we can. You'd better get business cards printed because you're going to need them."

"Thank you for giving me this opportunity, Dave. I can't tell you how much it means to me."

Christopher's stomach clenched as he witnessed the friendliness between his wife and Hedgewick. He didn't like it. Not at all. "Jenny, don't you think we should be going?"

Hedgewick released her hand. "I didn't mean to hold

you up. You probably want to celebrate on your own. I'll call you tomorrow and let you know what else sells.''

Christopher waited through a round of goodbyes, then escorted his wife to the car. When they'd buckled their seat belts, he asked, ''Would you like to stop somewhere to celebrate?''

''I'm not sure you're in the mood to celebrate,'' she said quietly. ''If you had business you wanted to take care of tonight, you should have just left instead of frowning impatiently most of the evening.''

''I didn't have business to take care of.''

''Then what was the problem? I've never been more excited or felt more fulfilled. The show was a success!''

''And so were you.''

''What's that supposed to mean?''

He switched on the ignition. ''Never mind.''

After a prolonged moment, she said, ''Fine. I'll never mind. Because I'd really like to savor tonight, not spoil it.''

In spite of what Jenny had said about savoring the evening, the silent drive home with Christopher took the bubbles out of her joy. She wished he'd just tell her what was wrong instead of acting like a volcano ready to erupt.

They'd built a foundation this week, she'd hoped. During her lessons they'd talked and laughed and, once in a while, touched. She'd seen the desire in his eyes, but had also seen the protective shield he'd kept firmly in place. He still needed answers and so did she. But what if they never had the answers?

Christopher drove the car around back to the garage. They went through the kitchen; he'd strode halfway across the dining room when he stopped, turned, and faced her. ''Are you attracted to Hedgewick?''

''What?''

"Are you attracted to him? Do you like talking to him? Do you want to go to bed with him?"

She was so astonished by Christopher's questions, all she could do was shake her head. "You're being ridiculous."

He took her by the shoulders. "Am I? There were men there tonight who wanted you just like I do. And I understand that because you're a beautiful woman, vibrant and talented. But what I don't know is how you looked at them. *If* you looked at them. You and Hedgewick are so easy together—"

"Christopher! Dave is a nice man. He understands my vision…what I want to accomplish when I snap a picture. But that's all he is. *You* are my husband. *You're* the man I want."

His hands moved from her shoulders, up her neck, and into her hair. "I wish I could believe that."

"Believe it," she murmured, needing him to trust her and the future they could share.

Whether he trusted her or not, he kissed her. It was hungry and possessive and claiming, leaving no place for thought of anything or anyone but him. And she needed to show him there wasn't anything or anyone but him. Not even tonight. She let him master her, finally returning his fervor with demands of her own.

When his fingers fumbled with the zipper at the back of her dress, she let him skate it down, then she reached for his tie. As she tugged it open, he pushed her dress from her shoulders. It dropped to the floor. She stepped out of it and started on his buttons while he shrugged off his jacket. She couldn't think or speak while he unhooked her bra and caressed her breasts, his gaze on hers. Not avoiding the fire in his eyes or his need, she ran her fingers up his ribs, glorying in his shudder.

"Dammit, Jenny. I don't want to need you this much," he growled as he closed his eyes.

"Need me, Christopher. Because I need you."

With concise, quick movements, he ridded her of her half slip and pantyhose, after which he pulled her tightly against him for another mind-bending kiss. Caught up in the momentum, she wrapped her arms around his neck, and he lifted her until her legs wound about him. His hands moved feverishly up and down her back until he set her on the buffet, stripped off his trousers and briefs, then pulled her toward him and entered her with a swift thrust.

"Say my name," he ordered her, staring into her eyes, letting her know he wouldn't go any further until she told him she knew exactly who he was.

"Christopher." His name rang out clear. When he thrust again, she cried for him again, urging him on, assuring him she wanted his passion and their marriage.

Explosively she climaxed around him, and as he drove to his release, he made her his and his alone.

As they clung to each other in the aftershock, the phone on the buffet rang, startling them both.

Christopher raised his head with an oath and pulled away. "It's after midnight," he said gruffly. "Maybe you should get that. I wouldn't want someone to hang up because they reached the wrong party."

His suspicions again. And she couldn't tell him he was wrong. Someone could very well know her husband often worked late and she'd be alone in the house. When she picked up the receiver and answered, she held her breath.

"Jenny, it's Marjorie. Can I speak to Christopher?" There was a tremor in her mother-in-law's voice. Jenny handed the phone to her husband. "It's your mother."

He took the receiver and as he listened, his face paled. "I'll be right over. There are some people I can call. I'll find out what's going on." When he hung up, he said, "Dad left Indiana tonight and no one's heard from him. Apparently an unexpected storm front moved in. I'm going to the study to make some calls, then I'll head over."

Jenny grasped his arm before he could move away from her. "I'm coming with you."

"It's not necessary."

"I'm your wife, Christopher. I care about you and your family. I'm coming along."

Avoiding her gaze, he pulled away and picked up their clothes, handing hers to her. "All right. But I'll be ready to leave in ten minutes."

Before she realized his intent, he'd lifted her from the buffet and set her on the floor. Then he was gone, leaving her heart and mind swirling in a sea of emotions.

As soon as Jenny saw Marjorie, she hugged her. "How are you doing?"

Marjorie gave her a tight squeeze in return. "I'm so worried." She turned to her son. "Did you find out anything?"

He draped his arm around his mother's shoulders and led her to the sofa in her living room. "Dad filed a flight plan and took off around eight p.m. He was supposed to land in Pittsburg to refuel but didn't. An unexpected weather front moved in throughout that area. There was no distress call but if he was trying to maneuver..."

"He might not have gotten one out before the plane went down," his mother finished, almost in tears.

Jenny sat on Marjorie's other side and held her hand. "You don't know that for sure."

"They're checking airfields. He could have put down anywhere," Christopher offered optimistically, though Jenny could see the worry he was trying to hide. "The weather is preventing visibility for a search. We're doing all we can for now. We just have to wait."

"But if he's all right, why doesn't he radio in?" Marjorie asked. "You think he crashed, don't you? Be honest with me."

"I don't know any more than I'm telling you. Dad's an experienced pilot. We have to trust his skill."

Silent tears slipped down Marjorie's cheeks. "Why didn't he wait until morning?"

Jenny squeezed her mother-in-law's hand. "He probably just wanted to get home."

"Are you sure we can't do anything but wait?" Christopher's mother asked him.

"That's all we can do."

Marjorie seemed to pull herself together as she rose from the sofa. "Then I'm going to make us tea."

"Would you like some help?" Jenny asked.

Marjorie managed a smile. "That would be nice. I'm sorry I ruined a special night for you. I'm glad you came with Christopher."

"You didn't ruin anything. While we're waiting for the water to boil you can remind me of any odds and ends I might have forgotten for the auction. Friday night will be here before we know it."

Marjorie looked grateful for a tangible subject to focus on. "I made a list. We'll get it on the way to the kitchen. Christopher, would you like something to eat? We could make some sandwiches."

"No, Mother. I'm going to make a few more calls." His gaze met Jenny's.

She wanted to go to him and hug him. But since their frenzied lovemaking and the phone call, he'd been miles away. She was beginning to wonder if her love for him was enough or if they'd need a miracle to bring them back together.

The feel of something on Jenny's shoulder awakened her. She was curled on the love seat, and Christopher had pulled a blanket up to her chin. "Thank you. What time is it?"

"Around two."

Jenny sat up. When she couldn't keep her eyes open, Christopher and his mother's voices had been murmuring in the background. "Any word yet?"

He shook his head and sank down beside her. "Nothing. And it's difficult to search before daylight. If he did crash…"

She put her hand over his, particularly mindful of the wedding band he wore. "Where's Marjorie?"

"She went to the kitchen to make another cup of tea—"

When the phone rang, Marjorie came running into the room. Christopher jumped up, going to the end table by the sofa. When he snatched up the phone, he listened, and then he smiled. After a few moments, he handed the receiver to his mother. "It's Dad."

Marjorie grabbed the phone. "Wayne. Wayne, are you all right?"

Christopher crossed to Jenny. "Lightning hit the plane. He went down in the middle of nowhere and had to walk pretty far for help. Apparently he was unconscious for a while and he thinks his arm is broken. The people at the farmhouse where he ended up insisted on calling an ambulance before he called here."

Jenny hopped up and hugged her husband, burying her nose in his neck, letting the tears of relief come. "I'm so glad."

His arms slowly enfolded her as he hugged her back. But

then he pulled away. "I'm going to make some calls on the cell phone."

Marjorie was still speaking to her husband when the paramedics arrived at the farmhouse. She insisted on talking to one of them before she hung up. Afterward she told Christopher and Jenny it could be a few hours until they admitted Wayne to the closest hospital and thoroughly checked him out. She wanted to immediately fly to Ohio where he'd crashed, but her husband had ordered her and Christopher to stay at home and wait for his call. Then she asked if her son and daughter-in-law would like to get some sleep upstairs. Christopher declined, saying they'd wait for her to call them at home.

When Jenny glanced at Christopher's profile in the car, he looked as wrung out as she felt. After he parked in the drive and they went in the front door, Jenny preceded him up the steps.

"I called Luke and told him what happened," Christopher said. "He'll be waiting to hear from us. I'll call Jud when we know for sure how Dad is."

Jenny walked down the hall ahead of her husband and stood at the door to the master suite. He stopped when he reached it and looked down at her. "You were terrific with Mother. Thank you for trying to distract her."

She shook her head. "No thanks are necessary." Grasping her courage in both hands, she asked, "Christopher, why don't you come in and sleep with me?"

His brows arched. "Sleep?"

"Yes. We both need it. And I think we need each other, too. Don't you?"

He stared at her for a moment, then brushed the back of his hand down her cheek. "Life is so fragile, isn't it?"

When she nodded, he dropped his hand and opened the door to the bedroom.

She changed into her nightgown in the bathroom. When she approached the bed, she saw Christopher had already turned back the covers and crawled in. When she lifted the sheet and slid under it, she realized he was naked.

"Isn't this what you wanted?" he asked, his voice gruff.

His expression was unreadable, and she knew she had to reach his heart somehow. "I want you to trust me. I want you to trust our marriage and our ability to build a future together."

He propped himself on his elbow and his tone was stern when he spoke. "What if I trust you, Jenny? Even if I could forget you turned to another man, how do I know you won't do it again?"

Moving closer to him, she vowed, "I can promise you. I can pledge my fidelity to you. I don't know what happened in the past, but I can control what I do in the future."

"What happens if I believe you, if I trust you and we begin rebuilding our marriage, then you *do* remember what happened and decide you'd rather spend your life with him rather than me?"

So *this* was the real issue between them. He didn't trust the woman she'd been or the woman she was now. "I don't know how to answer you because I'm not sure you'll believe anything I say."

"Try me."

She wasn't only fighting for her marriage but for her love and life with this man. Yet she was certain words of love and promises wouldn't convince him he should let down his guard so she could get close to him again. Neither could she use the physical attraction between them because he would feel she was trying to manipulate him.

All she could do was speak the truth and tell him her dream. "I want to *be* with you, Christopher, in every way a husband and wife should be together. I want you to come home to me and tell me about your day, then listen to me tell you about mine. I want to go horseback riding with you, take you along with me when I shoot a roll of film. I want you to make love to me and let me make love to you, both of us giving and taking, holding each other through the good and the bad. And most of all, once you've decided if you want all of this, too, I'd like to start a family and have your babies.''

She could count each beat of her heart as she waited for his response. Not an emotion flickered in his eyes, but the nerve in his jaw worked so she knew he wasn't as unaffected as he might want her to believe.

Finally he said, ''You want a lot.''

''Maybe so. I've always had dreams. And I've always believed they can come true. Can't you believe, too? In me? In us?''

He pushed himself up and sat facing her. ''I don't know if I've ever believed or trusted anyone but Luke and Jud. You and I… We made our vows and I expected you to be faithful. I expected you to stay by my side.''

''Because we signed a contract?'' She felt hurt by what he'd said but glad he was opening up to her.

''Marriage *is* a contract,'' he said defensively.

''Marriage should be so much more than a contract. It should be more than two suitable people living together because it's convenient. I want more. The question is—do you?''

His chest rose and fell a few times before he answered. ''That's not the kind of question I can answer right now, or even in a few days or weeks.''

''So we live in limbo?'' she asked, wondering if they'd made any progress at all.

He took his time before answering. ''No. We take each day as it comes and we try to start over. Okay?''

With each new day, his trust in her would build. With each new day, she'd bind him to her with love until the words meant as much as her actions and she could say them freely, knowing he'd accept them. "Okay."

Raking his hand through his hair, he said, "I think the best way to start is with some sleep." Sliding down under the sheet, he lay on the pillow on his side of the bed, but then he opened his arm to her.

She moved close to him, laying her head on his shoulder, hoping for the best, dreaming of tomorrow.

Chapter Ten

Auction-goers meandered around the hotel ballroom Friday evening, stopping and examining items that interested them, from antique jewelry kept safe in a glass case to a three-foot ceramic replica of a German shepherd. Jenny checked her notes on the podium, making sure the note cards describing each item fell in the right sequence.

Someone tapped her on the shoulder and she turned to see Christopher's parents smiling at her. Wayne sported a cast on his right arm. A row of stitches lined the edge of his jaw along with a large bruise.

She wrapped her arms around him and gave him a huge hug. "I'm so glad to see you. How do you feel?"

He hugged her back then leaned away. "You mean since I had to fly home on a commercial airline? Or since the doctor in Ohio called my doctor here who informed my wife I was supposed to act like a couch potato for at least a few days? What a boring existence. And those lines at the airport—"

Marjorie smiled. "He's grouchy because he can't go into work until Monday."

"I'm lucky she let me out tonight," he grumbled.

Jenny swallowed a laugh. "I'm glad you could come." Then her laughter slipped away. "Even more glad that you're here and safe. Any chance we can weatherproof you in the future?"

"Wait till you see the gizmos the new plane will have."

Jenny glanced at her mother-in-law to see how she felt about her husband flying again. "I can't keep him on the ground," Marjorie said with a resigned sigh. "But would you believe he agreed to take a cruise to Greece with me in the fall?"

Wayne took his wife's hand. "When the lightning struck and the plane was going down, I decided a few more vacations with you every year wouldn't hurt."

Jenny had sensed a strong bond of respect and warmth between Christopher's parents before. It was even stronger now. Maybe there *was* a larger plan guided by a divine hand. Someday she'd figure out how *her* accident fit in.

When Christopher approached them, her heart tripped. The night of his father's accident, something had changed in their relationship. They slept in the same bed now. Her husband made love to her, and she made love to him with every fiber of her being. But afterward when she gazed into his eyes, she could still see doubts. Would time take them away?

Or would his suspicions and her amnesia always be a specter between them?

She couldn't dwell on that. She had to focus on her love for him and his feelings for her, praying one day they would share the trust and marriage she longed for.

His gaze swept over her royal-blue suit trimmed in white and came to rest on the rings on her hand.

Sunday morning around five a.m., they'd awakened to the ringing of the phone. Marjorie had assured them Wayne would truly be all right and she was taking a flight out around noon to go be with him. Then Christopher had taken Jenny in his arms and they'd made love. She'd still felt his restraint, though, his desire to protect himself from feeling too much. When she'd dressed, she'd returned her rings to her finger to show him she was committed to their marriage. But in the past week he hadn't commented on them.

Switching his attention to his parents, Christopher smiled. "See anything you want to bid on?"

"There's a tapestry over there I wouldn't mind having for the upstairs hall. C'mon, Wayne. Let's go look at it and decide how high we should go."

Jenny's father-in-law rolled his eyes. "This feels a lot like shopping."

Christopher chuckled as his parents moved away. "He'll probably bid on more items than Mother will."

"I just hope I can do an adequate job of describing them and handling the bidding. I've been practicing all week. But now that I actually have to use the gavel, I'm more nervous than I expected to be. Look at all these people!"

Browsers filed into the rows of chairs with their numbers. The room was practically filled.

Christopher moved slightly closer to her. "You'll do fine. If you find yourself getting stage fright," he leaned toward her ear, "just imagine everyone in their underwear."

His breath was warm on her cheek, his aftershave as teasing as his body so close to hers. "If I imagine you in your underwear, I might not be able to continue with the auction," she murmured.

His smile told her that her sentiments pleased him. "I told Luke and his parents we'd join them and Mother and

Dad for coffee after the auction. Maybe we should make it a very quick cup.''

The usher in the back of the room closed the center double doors and waved at Jenny. She waved back, signaling she'd call the room to order. Christopher nodded to where his parents and the Hobarts sat in the front row on the right. ''If you need me to run up the price on an item, give me a nod.''

''You might get stuck with it,'' she warned.

''This is a good cause.''

Jenny watched her husband as he made his way to his seat. He smiled at several people he knew, stopping to shake a man's hand. His friends, colleagues and family were here tonight. She wanted to do a superb job of auctioneering so he'd be proud of her.

So he'd love her?

She knew she could earn his respect, but she wasn't sure anyone could earn love. Shuffling her note cards, she tapped them together on the podium and lifted the gavel to begin.

Once she'd given a welcome and brief introduction, she described one item after another, took bids, and cajoled her audience into offering more with her smile, with a few words about how the benefits from the auction would help children, with more creative attributes about the piece being auctioned. Every once in a while she looked at her husband, saw him watching her speculatively, and wondered what he was thinking.

After getting a particularly good price on a carnival glass dish, she took a few sips of water and waited for one of her helpers to set the next object on the table beside her for bids.

As Christopher listened to his wife's voice, he decided she'd never looked more alive...more beautiful. The rings on her finger sparkled as she moved her hand. Could he trust that they meant the same commitment to her that they meant to him? Would he ever trust her again? Could he forgive her?

When his pager beeped, he was almost glad. The same questions plagued him too often, and he was afraid he'd never have the answers. Checking the readout, he saw his home number. It must be an emergency for Pauline to page him here.

Excusing himself, he went to the lobby to the pay phone and dialed. Pauline picked up on the first ring.

"It's me, Pauline," he said.

"Mr. Langston, I didn't know whether to call you or not. A man was here. For Mrs. Langston. He was very determined and I...well, I told him where she was. I'm sorry, sir. Maybe I shouldn't have—"

Christopher's heart pounded. "Did he give his name?"

"Yes, sir. Martin Nesbitt."

Martin. Marty. Christopher realized he was soon going to face the shadow that had torn apart his marriage. "Describe him."

"Black hair. Blue eyes. Jeans and a plaid shirt..."

"I'll take care of it, Pauline. Don't worry. You were right to call me."

When he hung up, he thought about waiting in the lobby. But there were lots of men in jeans coming and going and he didn't want to make a mistake. With Jenny at the podium, there was no way anyone could get to her without Christopher spotting him. He'd go back inside...and wait.

As the minutes ticked by, he studied Jenny's face, his body tense. Maybe this Martin Nesbitt would wait for her outside. Maybe he wouldn't show up at all. He might not want to meet her in a public place. Yet, he'd boldly shown up at their home...

His wife was describing a hand-carved chess set when the center double doors at the rear of the room opened. Her gaze flicked from the bidding table to the newcomer. She went silent and stared. As the group gathered to bid realized she hadn't just paused but was mesmerized by something in the back, they murmured and turned.

Jenny's eyes widened, her hand went to her temple, and she let out a gasp. Christopher was on his feet and reached her side before the man coming up the side aisle could. All the anger, all the resentment, all the doubts that had caused him so much chaos in the past few months spurted out with his question. "Is this your lover?"

Tears came to Jenny's eyes and rolled down her cheeks as she didn't take her gaze from the man in jeans walking toward her. "This man is my father." And with those words she swayed. Christopher's shock immobilized him, and Martin Nesbitt caught his daughter in his arms.

Marjorie was beside Jenny instantly, directing Nesbitt to lay her down. She took her daughter-in-law's hand. "Jenny. Jenny, honey. You're going to be fine."

Jenny's eyes fluttered open and her hand went to her forehead. "I feel so funny...dizzy...a headache." She looked away from Marjorie to the man she'd said was her father. "Marty. What are you...? I was in an accident after I left you. I couldn't remember. When I saw you just now, everything came rushing back."

As if she suddenly remembered where she was, she looked up at Christopher. "Oh my gosh. What a scene I've caused. I'm so sorry..."

Christopher felt as if he'd been hit on the head with a building. He had so many questions, overwhelming guilt, yet he couldn't think of himself, he had to think of her. "I'll call Dr. Coswell. Don't move her until I get back," he ordered no one in particular yet everyone in sight.

The next hour was a blur as the doctor's service contacted her and she returned Christopher's call. While he was still on the phone with her in the lobby, Jenny walked toward him, her hand still rubbing her temple, Martin Nesbitt close by her side.

"I told you to keep her still..." Christopher warned.

Jenny stepped up to him and put out a shaking hand for the phone. Seeing her determination, realizing no one could have kept her still, he handed it to her. She answered a few questions, then hung up. "Dr. Coswell is going to meet me at the house."

"I'll get the car," Christopher said, not knowing what else to do.

Marjorie insisted on staying with Jenny, holding her hand, protecting her daughter-in-law from anyone who might ask questions or upset her further—including Christopher—by sitting beside her in the back seat. Martin Nesbitt drove Christopher's father to the house. Though Wayne waited in the living room, Martin followed his daughter upstairs. Marjorie accompanied Jenny to her bedroom, closing the door until Dr. Coswell arrived. When she stayed in the room with Jenny and the doctor, Christopher supposed his wife wanted her there.

He rubbed his hand up and down the back of his neck, staring at the closed bedroom door, feeling shell-shocked. As his gaze locked with Martin Nesbitt's where he sat on the settee in the upstairs hall, he didn't know what to say. He guessed that someone had already filled in Jenny's father on the extent of her accident and her memory loss.

"So...you're Christopher Langston," Nesbitt drawled. "Jenny told me about you."

"She didn't tell me about you," Christopher admitted, his voice gruff.

"She was afraid to."

As Christopher really looked at Martin Nesbitt, the black hair and blue eyes, his facial features, he saw the resemblance between this man and his wife. "Why would she be afraid?"

"She didn't know what your attitude would be. She already felt you were on the verge of a divorce, and she was afraid if you knew about me, you'd think less of her and it would tip the scales."

"Divorce? Why would she think—?"

"Oh, I know your kind, Mr. Langston. Lots of money, lots of work, lots of business trips. The last one was going to be two months long, right? Jenny seemed to think that meant you didn't give a hoot about your marriage, let alone her."

"She said that?"

"If you knew your wife, you'd know she'd *never* say that. Too loyal. But I could read between the lines, even though I hadn't known her very long."

"I thought her father died when she was a teenager." Christopher was still trying to fit the pieces together.

Nesbitt patted the settee. "Have a seat. Unless you have a problem sitting next to an ex-con."

Christopher saw the challenge in Nesbitt's eyes and met it, sitting beside him, saying, "Tell me what I should know."

The older man eyed him harshly for a moment, then let out a sigh. "The way I understand it, this past October Jenny found a letter I wrote to her mother from prison. Lydia and I were involved when she was twenty-one and in college. She and I never belonged together. She was too high-class. Wanted to be a lawyer. So I guess I decided I could get her things she wanted the easy way. I embezzled funds where I worked, wrote bad checks...and I got caught. While I sat in jail, she found out she was pregnant."

"But your name isn't on Jenny's birth certificate."

"Back here in Hartford, a friend of Lydia's family was sweet on her, even though he was fifteen years older. She'd known him all her life. He was a doctor, the kind of man she should have gotten involved with in the first place. They got married and his name went on Jenny's birth certificate when she was born. Lydia wrote me about it. I'd ruined *my* life, the best thing I could do for her was get out of hers. I agreed never to get in touch with her again."

"Jenny never knew."

"Not till she read the letter."

"How did she find you?"

"A private investigator. He traced me through prison records."

"*When* did she find you?"

"She first called me in February. We spent lots of time on the phone. But I had strict orders to hang up if you answered. She wanted to tell you. Kept waiting for the right time. Then you informed her you were leaving for two months. She felt she had to meet me face to face, spend some time with me, so she could tell you before you left."

"She was with you those four days."

"Yep. In a small town outside of Corning. I own a diner now. Jenny saw I have an honest life." He took a folded sheet of paper from his shirt pocket. "Here's the letter she found. She gave it back to me for safekeeping. I think maybe you need to see it."

Christopher took the yellow paper and skimmed it, not attempting to push away the remorse and regrets flooding through him. "I thought she was having an affair. I've been judging her, treating her as if she'd been unfaithful. If our marriage was in trouble before, I've probably destroyed it now. I can't believe I was so blind!"

Jenny's father looked him over pensively. "Nothing I

say is going to make you feel better. I was beginning to think you were a real bastard, leaving her here alone night after night, only being with her when it was convenient for you.''

Christopher swallowed hard because what Jenny's father thought was true. ''I was. If she couldn't even tell me she'd found a father she didn't know she'd had, I don't deserve her.''

Nesbitt shrugged. ''Seems to me that you were both making some mistakes.''

Christopher's heart ached from all the wrong decisions he'd made, let alone the conclusions he'd drawn. ''She won't see it that way. Not now that she can remember everything. She's wanted to rebuild our marriage, and I've treated her as if she'd done something unforgivable.''

''I haven't known my daughter very long, but I do know she loved you.''

Christopher realized now that he hadn't cherished that love, he'd simply taken it for granted. How could she forgive him for that, let alone his doubts and suspicions?

The door to the bedroom opened and Dr. Coswell and Marjorie emerged. His mother closed the door behind her, then smiled at Martin Nesbitt. ''Why don't you and I go downstairs? I know you drove my husband here, but the three of us should get properly introduced.''

Waiting until his mother and Jenny's father went downstairs, Dr. Coswell finally spoke. ''Your wife is sleeping. I gave her a mild sedative.''

''Is she all right?''

The doctor lifted her black bag and tucked it under her arm. ''She will be. She has a monumental headache. But I think sleep will help that. Tonight was traumatic for her. When her father stepped into that room, everything converged like an avalanche rushing toward her. She remembered him and the accident, as well as the years since her graduation.''

''She didn't ask to see me.'' He was afraid that was a sign she'd given up on him and their marriage.

Mary Coswell gave him a compassionate smile. ''Give her some time to sort things out. Her emotions and the resurgence of memories exhausted her. She'll be better able to talk about and deal with them after a good night's sleep. I told her to call me tomorrow and let me know how she feels.''

As Christopher walked Dr. Coswell down the steps to the door, he could only think about his sleeping wife upstairs. Going into the living room, he felt as if he needed a good stiff drink. Yet he knew liquor would never numb the ache that told him he might have lost Jenny for good. With a perception Christopher appreciated, his mother asked Martin Nesbitt to spend the night at their house. He accepted.

Finally Christopher stood in the foyer alone, lost in the silence, tormented by regrets. Jenny needed to sleep, but he needed to be beside her, just in case he wouldn't have the chance again. He climbed the stairs and carefully opened the door to their bedroom. With a pain in his heart so great he didn't think it would ever diminish, he knew he couldn't lie beside her. She might not want him there. So as quietly as he could, he moved the chair over by the bed, and he sank into it, never letting his gaze leave her face.

The first song of birds playing on the spout outside her room awakened Jenny. Keeping her eyes closed, she realized the terrible headache was gone. It had hit her in the same blinding flash as her memories when she'd seen her father walk into the ballroom.

Her father.

Marty.

The letter she'd found in the attic among her mother's papers had been a terrible shock, shaking the foundations of her identity. The father she'd admired and loved while she was growing up wasn't truly her father. Her mother had kept the secret all her life. Because she was ashamed of the affair that had gotten her pregnant? Because she was ashamed of Marty Nesbitt?

Those weeks of not knowing whether or not to search for her biological father had caused such turmoil. But once Jenny had hired the private investigator, she'd known she couldn't turn back. She'd liked Marty from their first phone conversation. But she'd been so afraid to tell Christopher...

Christopher.

What could he be thinking? She'd kept the secret for months, afraid she'd lose him if she told him about her true origins. He'd married her because of who he'd thought she was. Her parents' social status had been part of her identity. The scene last night flashed behind her closed eyelids. Christopher's family, his friends and colleagues had witnessed everything. They all knew her father wasn't a doctor, but...

The man who had raised her *was* a doctor and a fine man. He might not have been her natural father, but he'd been a good father and she'd love him always. Yes, Marty Nesbitt, her biological father was an ex-convict. So what? Even if gossip had already started, she had to remind herself she had nothing to be ashamed of. Before she'd hired the P.I., the idea of having an ex-convict for a father had frightened her to death. But she'd gotten to know Marty and had seen how he'd turned his life around. She was proud of him. And if Christopher didn't feel that way, if he couldn't accept who she really was, then, as much as she loved him, maybe they didn't belong together.

She'd been too unnerved to face him last night, knowing she'd probably see disapproval on his face, anger because she hadn't told him about her father. But she wasn't unnerved now. Opening her eyes, ready to throw back the sheet and find Christopher...

She froze. Her husband was sitting in a chair by the bed, his head tilted against the back, his stocking feet propped on the mattress. His tie lay on the floor on top of his shoes. A beard stubble shadowed his jaw, his hair looked disheveled, and he'd opened the top two buttons of his shirt and turned back his shirt cuffs.

She must have made some kind of sound because he opened his eyes and sat up in the chair. With him studying her so intensely, she knew she had to plow right in. "I'm sorry about last night, and I'm sorry I didn't tell you about my father. I was afraid I'd lose you."

A bird chirped into the silence.

"Did you ever really know you had me? Or my love?" Christopher asked.

Unexpectedly her eyes filled with tears.

Leaning forward, he took her hand almost tentatively, as if afraid she'd pull away. "You don't have any reason to be sorry. I do. Too many reasons to count. Maybe too many for you to forget, let alone forgive. I took you and our marriage for granted. I never realized until your accident that a marriage needs care and nurturing to grow. I never realized that I was closing you out, guarding myself against the kind of intimacy I sensed you wanted. I spent hours last night, watching you, thinking about how I failed you as a husband."

"Christopher, you didn't fail me. I just wasn't brave enough—"

"I failed you," he said, his voice low and deep. "If you

had known that I truly loved you, you could have told me about your father. Both fathers.''

Sitting up and sliding toward him, she knew she couldn't let him take all the blame. "I should have told you I was lonely. I should have told you I was afraid to have children because I didn't know if our marriage was strong enough to give them the love and support they'd need. I shouldn't have put my dreams aside and depended so much on you.''

With a shake of his head, he looked deep into her eyes. "I've loved you, Jenny, probably from the first conversation we ever had. But I never told you enough, if I told you at all. I guess I thought my desire showed you. But then when I started believing…'' He cleared his throat. "I'm so sorry I doubted you. I don't have any excuse except maybe I really doubted myself. Deep down, I knew I wasn't loving you enough.''

Her love for her husband overflowed. She'd fallen in love with him because of his strength of character, and she'd never seen it more clearly than at this moment. "What is enough?'' she asked softly.

After thinking about it, he said, "Enough is putting your dreams and desires *beside* mine, not behind them. Enough is spending time with you to simply *be* together whether you're shooting a roll of film or sitting beside me watching a movie. Enough is raising children who will be honest and caring and who will know how to trust much better than I have.''

He looked uncertain and so vulnerable, as if she still might turn him away. She never could. Not in this life or the next. "I love you, Christopher. Will you make love to me?''

The tension on his face eased. Still holding her hand, he brought her palm to his lips and kissed it so tenderly, her tears threatened to surface again.

He stood, then lay on the bed beside her, stroking her hair away from her cheek. "I have a theory that after your accident, you blocked out me and our marriage because I didn't love you well enough. I promise you that for the next fifty or sixty years at least, you will never, ever, forget how much I love you."

Jenny slipped her arms around her husband. As he kissed her, her fervor told him she believed every word of his promise and vowed the same love in return.

Epilogue

On June eighth, Jenny stood in the dining room in her off-white crepe dress with its long chiffon sleeves, satin cuffs and collar and cropped jacket, feeling every bit as much a bride as she had on her wedding day. Guests had gathered under the canopy in the garden to watch her and Christopher renew their wedding vows.

Her father stood outside the dining room's sliding glass doors, waiting patiently for her. Today was her father's birthday, the numbers 6/8 she'd written on the slip of paper that she'd found in her wallet. This day had seemed perfect for their celebration since Marty had truly brought her and Christopher together.

"Ready to get married?" Christopher grinned as he came toward her in his black tux, a package in his hand.

"Remarried," she amended.

He lifted her chin and gave her a kiss that was as thorough as it was quick. "A present came from Jud. But it just has your name on it. There was a note with it for both of us, though. He said he's sorry he can't be here but we should come visit soon. He has his hands full with Uncle Thatcher and training the two-year-olds. I think he puts them in the same category.''

Taking the shirt-sized box from Christopher that was wrapped in wedding-bell wrap with a silver bow, she tore open the side of the paper and pulled out the present. When she lifted the lid, she found a loop of rope tied with one very serious knot.

''That's a strange vow-renewal celebration present, don't you think?'' Christopher asked.

With everything that had happened and her newfound happiness with her husband, she'd forgotten about her conversation with Jud. She smiled, thinking about it. ''After we returned from New York and heard Marty's message, you were very upset.''

''I remember,'' Christopher admitted with a grimace. ''But I wish you didn't.''

''I never want to forget another thing,'' she reminded him with a kiss on his cheek that told him again she'd more than forgiven him. ''Anyway, I called Jud for some advice.''

''Jud?''

''Don't sound so surprised. I felt he liked me and would listen to me.''

''As opposed to Luke who believed what I told him? You were right to call Jud. He insisted you'd never have an affair.''

''Luke was just being loyal to you. I understand that. And, Jud. He helped. He told me to rope you and hog-tie you if that's what it took to get you to listen to me.''

Christopher chuckled. ''Jud knows me well.'' He took the rope from the box and handed it to her. ''Do you think you'll need it?''

She gazed up at her husband, loving the openness in his

eyes, loving the tenderness on his face, loving him.
"Nope." Pressing it into his hand, she asked, "What do
you think we should do with it?"

With a wink, he answered, "I'll hang it in my office so
I remember to listen. Though being roped and hog-tied by
you might be a lot of fun."

Christopher's lighter side had been emerging more and
more lately. Though the desire between them was anything
but light. "Are you going to tell me where we're going on
our second honeymoon?" He'd kept their destination to
himself, telling her he wanted to surprise her.

"Do you really want to know?"

"You told Pauline what she should pack for me. But I
might want to add a few things."

"Tonight we're staying at a five-star hotel—you won't
need anything for that." His grin was thoroughly sexy and
reminded her of every night they'd shared, and some afternoons, since the auction. "Then, tomorrow," he continued, "we fly to Curaçao."

"Curaçao?" she repeated, thoroughly delighted. "How
wonderful!"

He circled her waist with his arm and nuzzled her neck.
"A tropical paradise, a bridal suite, and time to make love,
swim, and count the stars. But before we can go on a second honeymoon we have a few friends and family waiting
outside to witness us renew our vows."

Looking forward to every moment of the future with
Christopher, Jenny watched him lay the rope safely on the
buffet. Then he opened the sliding glass door and they
stepped out onto the patio. He escorted Jenny as far as the
white runner where she took her father's arm, and Marjorie
handed her a bouquet of pink roses and babies' breath.
Then Christopher walked his mother to her chair and stood
to the side of the minister, facing Jenny.

Marty smiled down at his daughter. "He's a good guy."

Her father and Christopher had spent some time together, playing golf, barbecuing on a new grill her husband had insisted on buying for the patio. They were actually enjoying the patio now. The past few evenings, she and Christopher had relaxed on a lounge chair, kissing under the stars.

Agreeing with Marty's estimation of her husband, she said, "He's a very special guy. And I'm ready to marry him all over again."

A violinist began playing, and her father slowly walked her down the aisle. Jenny smiled at Luke and his parents, at Marjorie and Wayne, Fred and Pauline, at the other guests who had made their lives richer. When Marty placed her hand in her husband's, she kissed her father's cheek, then took her place beside Christopher.

The minister began, "We are gathered here to renew the marriage of Christopher and Jenny Langston."

Jenny looked up at her husband and smiled. He returned her smile and squeezed her hand, mouthing the words, "I love you." She did the same, then they faced forward together, knowing they were looking in the same direction, believing that love would unite them for all time.

* * * * *

The next book in the
Do You Take This Stranger?
series is coming next month.
Watch for Jud's story in
LOVE, HONOR AND A PREGNANT BRIDE—*only*
from Silhouette Romance
in October 1998.

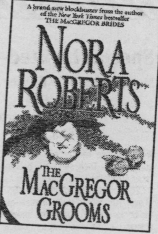
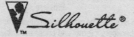

Take 2 bestselling love stories FREE

Plus get a FREE surprise gift!

Special Limited-Time Offer

Mail to Silhouette Reader Service™

> P.O. Box 609
> Fort Erie, Ontario
> L2A 5X3

YES! Please send me 2 free Silhouette Romance™ novels and my free surprise gift. Then send me 6 brand-new novels every month, which I will receive months before they appear in bookstores. Bill me at the low price of $3.25 each plus 25¢ delivery and GST*. That's the complete price, and a saving of over 10% off the cover prices—quite a bargain! I understand that accepting the books and gift places me under no obligation ever to buy any books. I can always return a shipment and cancel at any time. Even if I never buy another book from Silhouette, the 2 free books and the surprise gift are mine to keep forever.

315 SEN CH7T

Name	(PLEASE PRINT)

Address	Apt. No.

City	Province	Postal Code

This offer is limited to one order per household and not valid to present Silhouette Romance™ subscribers. *Terms and prices are subject to change without notice. Canadian residents will be charged applicable provincial taxes and GST.

CSROM-98

©1990 Harlequin Enterprises Limited

#1 *New York Times* bestselling author

NORA ROBERTS

Presents a brand-new book in the beloved MacGregor series:

THE WINNING HAND
(SSE#1202)

October 1998 in

Silhouette ® SPECIAL EDITION ®

Innocent Darcy Wallace needs Mac Blade's protection in the high-stakes world she's entered. But who will protect Mac from the irresistible allure of this vulnerable beauty?

**Coming in March, the much-anticipated novel,
THE MacGREGOR GROOMS
Also, watch for the MacGregor stories
where it all began!**

**December 1998:
THE MacGREGORS: Serena—Caine**

**February 1999:
THE MacGREGORS: Alan—Grant**

**April 1999:
THE MacGREGORS: Daniel—Ian**

Available at your favorite retail outlet, only from

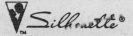

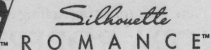

COMING NEXT MONTH

#1324 THE NINE-MONTH BRIDE—Judy Christenberry
Virgin Brides

It was supposed to be a marriage with just one objective—to make a baby! Or so Lucas Boyd and Susannah Langston thought. But the more time Susannah spent in Lucas's arms, the more he hoped to convince her that the real purpose was...love.

#1325 WEDDING DAY BABY—Moyra Tarling

They'd shared one passionate night eight months ago. But now naval officer Dylan O'Connor had no memory of that night—and Maggie Fairchild had an all-too-apparent reminder. Could Maggie rekindle their love before the stork arrived?

#1326 LOVE, HONOR AND A PREGNANT BRIDE
—Karen Rose Smith
Do You Take This Stranger?

Penniless and pregnant, young Mariah Roswell had come to rancher Jud Whitmore with the news of his impending fatherhood. But would the man who'd lovingly taken her virginity take her into his heart and make her his true-love bride?

#1327 COWBOY DAD—Robin Nicholas
Men!

Pregnant single mom Hannah Reese had learned the hard way that not all cowboys lived up to a code. Then she met rodeo star Devin Bartlett. Rough, rugged, reliable, he made her feel...and dream...again. Could *he* be the perfect cowboy dad—and husband?

#1328 ONE PLUS ONE MAKES MARRIAGE—Marie
Ferrarella
Like Mother/Like Daughter

Gruff Lancelot Reed never thought he'd love again—until Melanie McCloud came crashing into his life. Lance wanted to have nothing in common with this spirited woman, but the intense attraction he felt for her was more than even he could deny....

#1329 THE MILLIONAIRE MEETS HIS MATCH
—Patricia Seeley
Women To Watch

Millionaire Gabe Preston didn't know what to think of beautiful Cass Appleton when she landed on his property, searching for her missing cat. But as the fur flew between them, Gabe started hoping he could help her find something else—love.